MW00777342

THE *Shoes*

BY LILY HALL

Mary Jo,
Thank you so very
much! I hope you
LOVE my Story! -
Lily Hall

Paperclip Publishing, LLC
Chandler, AZ

The Shoes

Copyright © 2022 by Lily Hall

Published by: Paperclip Publishing LLC

Editor: Noelle S. LeBlanc
Cover Illustration & Design and Interior Typography: Hannah Thigpen

Library of Congress Control Number: 2022941031

ISBN: 979-8-88589-199-8 (paperback)

ISBN: 979-8-88589-198-1 (hardcover)

ISBN: 979-8-88589-190-5 (eBook)

Printed in Rephen Printing, Co. LTD in Guangzhou and the United States of America

First Printing: 2022

Paperclip Publishing LLC
3800 W Ray Road Suite 5
Chandler, AZ 85226

www.paperclippublishing.com

For my Dad. The stars always shone the brightest when you were here.

Contents

Prologue

"Do not worry, dear ones. It shall only be for a short time." The old man smiled lovingly as he placed each of the shoes into their dust bags. He then arranged them carefully in their box, taking the time to make sure they were padded and completely secure before he placed the cover back on top of the box.

"Before you know it, you will be with The Chosen, and you will be creating the most beautiful things together." A slight frown crossed his lips as he placed the box on the shelf, but a moment later he was all smiles once again. "It shall only be for a short time."

Shuffling slowly out of the room, he was careful to replace the opening just as he had found it. He knew the shoes would be safe there and this was the most important thing.

"And wherever The Chosen should go, the stars would follow..." He whispered the phrase softly to himself as he slipped out the front door. He paused to lock the door before shuffling quietly down the hallway.

Chapter 1

"Oh hey, did you hear?" asked Mr. Bronson as he nervously unstacked and restacked the display of enclosure cards for the flower arrangements by the register. "There's an out-of-towner looking for some person named after a star constellation or something. He's most definitely not from around here."

"Oh really?" Aunt Maggie asked as she handed him the bouquet of purple hyacinths he purchased. "How decidedly peculiar."

"Yeah definitely!" He smiled sheepishly at the purple flowers. "Well, I'm off to deliver these. Wish me luck! I'm sure I'll be seeing you again in a few days." It had become a weekly thing for Mr. Bronson to come into the flower shop to buy a bouquet of "I'm Sorry" flowers for his wife. They were newlyweds and he was bound and determined to start them off on the right foot.

Calli stepped out from the back room and shot her aunt a nervous look. "He was talking about me, huh?"

Maggie smiled brightly at her, "Oh, of course not, dear! He said the stranger was looking for someone named after a star constellation. Not a Greek muse!" She patted her arm and went back to arranging the pile of flowers she had been working on.

Calli sighed softly, unable to get rid of the feeling that something big was about to happen, but she decided to focus on the work at hand instead. They were prepping for a huge wedding that would be happening over the coming weekend and there was a ton of work still left to do.

When the abandoned barn next to her aunt's home had been listed for sale, Calli begged her aunt to help her purchase and remodel it for their flower shop. They were in a small shop on the main strip of the town they lived in, but they had grown out of it. Everything was incredibly cramped and they had little-to-no extra room. The purchase of the barn turned out to be perfect timing. Before they moved into the newly remodeled location, they ended up having to order a large shipping container with a refrigeration unit in it just to store all the orders for the various weddings they were booking.

Starting out as a large decrepit gambrel-style barn, they had to completely gut the inside, but the end result was well worth it. It turned into a location of pride in their small town, honoring the past while bringing it to current times.

The building was completely made of brick and had an overly large front door with two massive bay doors on each side. The bay doors were used for the different large farm machinery when it was in service. The original owner passed away, and the farm had become too much for the new owners. They sold various sections of the farm until the barn was on the last lot of land remaining.

Calli and her aunt had decided to keep the large openings of the bays in the front of the building, but due to the many years of disuse, the two large barn doors were no longer functional, so they had to find another solution. Instead of repairing the doors, they decided to reuse them as large tables on the main showroom floor.

For the now-empty bays, they installed a set of large steel bi-fold doors in them that included windows, so not only could potential customers see all the various flowers and items in the shop, but there was also a lot of natural light streaming in during the day. The best part about these doors was that they folded together like an accordion when opened, and because they opened so easily, Aunt Maggie left them open most days.

They had decided to keep the original heavy wood door that was centered between the two bay doors from the original barn but painted it a bright teal color instead of leaving the natural dark wood. It was now almost always propped open.

Calli's favorite part of the building, however, was the extra-large silo tower on the left side of the building that had been used as storage for grain. Calli loved that it was so tall and had a walkway built from her bedroom over to the tower. The builders had been able to create a small studio on the top floor of the silo. She also had them add a deck to the outside upper level where she would frequently sit and either stargaze or sketch.

She had tried to keep the showroom of the flower shop open and flowing, but her aunt eventually took over the area to the left of the register. A number of small buckets of flowers were set up on one of the sets of barn door tables. Throughout the day, people would come in and purchase the individual flowers to make their own bouquets, or her aunt would grab some of them to use in the bouquets she was making. It drove Calli a little bit crazy because of the clutter, but she generally just avoided that section of the shop.

On the other side of the register was the huge walk-in refrigerator with a sliding glass door. There they stored a variety of pre-made arrangements, and more loose flowers. Her aunt had been completely against the idea of adding the walk-in fridge when Calli first suggested it, but eventually she went along with it. It was a huge hit. Their customers liked being able to see all the different flowers they offered and select the perfect ones themselves.

She also added a section of various planters and vases on the second barn door table, so customers could pick and choose the perfect vase for their arrangement. Their customers were frequent visitors to the shop so she made sure to keep their showroom floor fresh. She had just added a variety of differently sized scented candles for sale from a local candle maker and she could hardly keep them in stock. Luckily by now, her aunt trusted Calli's ideas, and they were very successful together.

Her favorite items in the whole shop, however, were the set of dress forms located in the front windows. She had taken a variety of different silk flowers and designed dresses out of them. Because it was August and the end of the wedding season, there was one that was made only from white flowers such as peonies, roses, and lilies. The other one was inspired by summer and had a variety of brightly colored flowers like sunflowers, orange ranunculus, and bright pink dahlias. It had taken what seemed like forever to complete them, but they were definitely worth it. Morgan's Flowers was featured in several wedding magazines because of her flower dresses. The articles had brought a lot of customers from surrounding cities to their shop, and Calli was always very grateful for their increased popularity.

Her aunt was sitting at the table next to the registers, which was another area Calli did not touch. There were flowers and different sized containers scattered all over the top of it, spilling onto the floor. She loved her aunt, but Maggie was always in a constant state of chaos, be it her work area or her actual self.

Today, she was wearing a bright orange t-shirt that was several sizes too big with a pair of neon green leggings. The outfit might have looked okay on another person, but with her aunt's slight frame and the halo of flame-red hair, the colors just clashed.

There was no doubt that the two of them were related. They both had very similar facial features and were almost the same height, although Calli was just a little bit taller. They both had that wild red hair, but Calli kept hers meticulously tamed and always secure in a bun at the top of her head. She never wore it down to fly free like her aunt did. And she never wore the bright colors her aunt always seemed to favor. Calli's clothing palette ran more toward neutral colors like browns, greys, and black.

"This wedding will be so scrumptious," her aunt exclaimed as Calli came up next to her. "The bride and groom definitely know their flowers. I absolutely love working with peonies! They're my favorite flower by far!"

She laughed. Her aunt was decidedly excited about this wedding, which, in turn, made her happy. "I know, they're my favorite too. What needs to be done next, Aunt Maggie?" she asked.

"Well, I need this arrangement here to go to the refrigerator in the back because it's all done. And then, I'm going to take a lunch break if that's okay. I'll bring you back something super tasty, of course." Her aunt grinned. "I'll be back before you know it!"

"Okay, Aunt Maggie. I'll hold down the fort while you wrangle us up with some food." Calli knew that her aunt was actually sneaking away to go watch one of her soap operas, but since she lived right next to the flower shop, she knew she could always call her if anything happened. Besides, they were already ahead of schedule for the wedding so it would allow Calli some time to clean up around the shop. It was always in a state of constant chaos when her aunt was arranging, and this would give her the opportunity to organize everything. "And say hi to the doctors on your show for me." She winked at her aunt before gently pushing her out the door.

Calli was in the middle of pulling down some baby's breath from their overstock on top of the fridge area when she heard the bell ring to let her know someone had walked into the shop. "I'll be with you in just a moment," she said as she turned to smile apologetically at the new arrival.

When she realized it was not one of their frequent visitors, she stumbled on the stepladder. He was definitely not from anywhere near the little town they lived in. The dark grey shirt and pressed black slacks certainly stood out amongst the jeans and flannel the men in Clover, Oregon, typically wore. They all seemed to be channeling their inner loggers or hardcore weekend outdoor enthusiasts. This man was also clean shaven and well put together, whereas the men here took special pride in their beards.

"You're Calliope Morgan, aren't you?" he asked as he stepped a little further into the shop.

This question made Calli lose her grip on the massive box of baby's breath she was holding, and as she struggled to catch it, she misplaced her foot on the ladder. She teetered precariously on the edge of the stepladder, but the box was heavier than she had realized and it ended up bashing into her as it fell from the shelf, knocking her clean off the ladder.

A high-pitched squeal slipped out as she felt herself falling backward, but a moment later she found herself secure in the stranger's arms. Her face flushed as she realized how very close they were.

He seemed a tad in shock as he stared at her, his hazel eyes a little bit too wide. "Oh...hi."

"Hi, um, thanks for catching me? Could you put me down now please?"

"Oh yeah, of course! Sorry..." He said this a little too loudly as he set her down quickly. He straightened his already straight shirt as he peered down at her. "So, you're Calliope then, aren't you?"

"Yep... That's me, but most people around here know me as Calli." She started dusting the teeny flowers and stems from her shirt and hair. They had gotten everywhere.

"You know, you do look just like her...just a bit shorter."

"Um, thanks?" She laughed nervously, unsure of whom the 'her' he was referring to was. "So, what brings you to Clover? We aren't exactly a major tourist destination or anything."

Stepping closer to her, he reached over and gently touched her hair. "Here, you forgot some." She froze while he pulled the tiny flowers from her hair.

"Oh my goodness, Calli! What ever have you done? What a grand mess you've made! I swear! I can't leave you alone for more than two seconds—" her aunt said, stopping mid-sentence when she caught sight of the stranger. "Oh! Why hello there! What can we do for you, young man?"

Calli blushed and stepped away from the man. "This must be that stranger Mr. Bronson mentioned earlier today. Turns out he was looking for me after all." She looked at her aunt pointedly. "Although, he hasn't told me why he's been looking for me yet."

The man smiled at her aunt. "You must be Margaret Morgan. I've heard so much about you."

Aunt Maggie squinted at him and stood a little bit straighter. "Oh, really? From whom exactly?" She plucked a stray hair from her over-sized t-shirt and squared her shoulders to him. Seeing her tiny aunt standing up to this almost-a-foot-taller gentleman was enough to bring a smirk to Calli's lips.

"Oh, please forgive me. My name is Derrick Adams. I was sent here by Xander." He cleared his throat softly, "Excuse me, Alexander Verona. Calliope's father."

Aunt Maggie made a little gasping noise and turned to Calli. "Oh dear!"

Calli could see her aunt was distressed and went over to her. "What is he talking about? I've never even met my father. For all I know he may be dead."

"My goodness! I'm going to need to sit down…" Her aunt plopped down right where she was, but luckily there was a stool right behind her.

"Aunt Maggie, please tell me what's going on." Calli knelt by her aunt shooting anxious looks between her and the stranger.

Derrick cleared his throat. "I know this may come as a shock to you, but your father needs you to return to New York. It's about your mother's estate."

Calli stood up and walked over to Derrick forcefully. "Look, I don't know who you are, who my supposed father is, or what he wants me to do in New York, but I am not going anywhere. I will not leave my aunt."

Derrick nodded solemnly. "She said you would say that."

"Who said I'd say what?"

"Your mother." He reached into the black messenger bag that was slung across his shoulder and pulled out a large envelope.

"There's a plane ticket, a letter from your father, and a letter from your mother in this folio. I do hope you will decide to come." He gave her a brief smile as he handed her the large envelope and then retreated out of the flower shop.

Up in her apartment, Calli set the playlist on her iPod to her favorite mix of songs and cranked the stereo as loud as it could possibly go.

Once the music was playing, she made her way to the walk-in closet. She turned on the overhead light and walked to the back of the closet, stopping when she came to a very tall leather-covered wooden trunk.

She had inherited it after her mother passed away. She wasn't sure how her mother had come into possession of such an interesting trunk, but she was very happy to have it.

It was an old Louis Vuitton–monogrammed shoe trunk. Instead of sitting lengthwise and having the lid open up over it like most trunks, this trunk sat on one of its ends and opened out towards the person, more like a door than a lid. The trunk, which she had aptly named *The Beast*, came up to almost her breastplate when she was standing barefoot in front of it.

Undoing the clasps along the left side of the trunk, she carefully pulled the lid on its hinges toward her. Setting the folio from Derrick on the carpet next to her, she sat down in front of The Beast.

The inside of the trunk was another curiosity. Instead of an open space for storing clothes or other items, it has a slim drawer at the bottom of the space, an open tray area at the top, and twenty individual boxes in between. Each of the individual boxes has its own leather pull-tabs and a small customizable placard. It almost resembled an old school card catalog found in libraries that had not yet been updated to computers. The trunk was clearly worthy of holding her most prized possessions.

Calli touched the plaque nearest her with her mother's dainty-yet-broad handwriting. 'Benedetto', it read.

She pulled the small box out and set it on the floor next to her. She took a deep breath, the old musky scent of the trunk mixing with the newer leather aroma of the contents of each box enveloped her. It instantly worked its magic, and she could feel all the tension leave her body as she let out a slow breath.

Lifting the lid of the small box she had pulled out, she smiled as she thought about the contents of the box. These were by far her favorite.

Carefully, she moved the piece of satin covering the contents like a hidden treasure. A soft sigh escaped her lips as she pulled out the most beautiful pair of black high-heeled shoes. This pair of leather Benedettos were the most coveted pair of shoes from her mother's collection. Benedettos were notoriously hard to come by as the designer had stopped releasing new shoes several years ago. Calli had tried for the longest time to obtain another pair, but they were always just out of her price range.

She also had several pairs of her mother's Manolos, as well as a few classic pairs made by Roger Vivier, Beth Levine, Giuseppe Zanotti, and Salvatore Ferragamo. She even had a pair of the crazy heel-less high heels made by Andre Perugia. Luckily, she and her mother wore the same size shoe.

She had added several of her own pairs to the collection as well. Setting the Benedettos carefully on the ground, she briefly touched the plaques with names written in her own handwriting: Christian Louboutin, Yves Saint Laurent, Miu Miu, Jimmy Choo, Lanvin, Charlotte Olympia, Valentino, Nicholas Kirkwood, and Patrick Cox. Oh, all her new loves were there happily stored in their own little boxes.

Turning her attention back to the Benedettos, she slipped them carefully onto her bare feet. She focused on her reflection in the mirror she had attached to the lid of The Beast with velcro, taking time to admire the way her feet looked in the shoes. She rolled up the simple black pants she was wearing so that the shoes would be viewable before turning her attention to the folio.

First, she opened the letter from her father. It was very short, simple, and to the point:

Calliope,

Please come to New York. I look forward to getting to know you finally.

- Alexander

Wow. Ok, great first impression, Dad.

She was not sure what exactly she had been expecting, hearing from her father for the first time ever in her life. But this certainly was not it.

Calli shrugged with a sigh and turned to the letter from her mother. The handwriting was instantly recognizable, just from seeing her name on the envelope. Tracing her mother's handwriting on the envelope softly, her thoughts turned to one of their last moments together.

Her mother is sitting at her makeup table as Calli hides behind the open door to her mother's room. It is almost like watching an artist painting a masterpiece, she imagines, except the makeup is the paint and her stunning mother is already beautiful. She is just highlighting her striking beauty with the makeup.

Suddenly, her mother starts coughing loudly into a handkerchief. Calli holds her own breath for as long as she can, counting the seconds until her mother is able to breathe normally. Her mother is not aware she is standing in the doorway, and she frowns at the blood standing out starkly against the white of the handkerchief in her hand.

Calli sees the blood and gasps loudly, "Oh, Momma! You are sick! Please don't go to the party. Please stay home with me in bed."

"Oh, my darling, it is okay," her mother says as she motions to her to come closer. "This is a very important party and I must go. But do not worry, dear one, as I will be right as rain tomorrow."

"But, Momma, I'm scared."

"It will be fine, my darling, you will see." Her mother wraps her arms around her and kisses her on the forehead.

But, of course, it was not fine. The next morning, her beautiful, loving mother was admitted to the hospital. The cancer that had started in her breast had spread to her lungs. A week later, she had slipped into a coma, and a few days after that, she slipped away entirely.

Calli wiped the tears from her eyes and took a deep breath before opening her mother's letter.

My Dearest Calliope,

I very much wish this letter finds you well and happy. I hope life with your Aunt Margaret has gone smoothly. I love my darling sister, but I know she is not always on top of things.

I am so incredibly sorry for how things have turned out and hope you forgive me for leaving you much too soon. I suppose God needed some fashion advice and thought I was the best woman for the job.

I do hope that you accept your father's invitation and that you will begin the relationship I know you both need. Please do not blame him for not contacting you before now. It was my wish that you grow up unfettered to the life I led in New York and, unfortunately, he was a part of that life.

He may seem closed off in the beginning, but please just give him time. He is a wonderfully kind man.

If you do decide to return to New York, you will have full access to my apartments and work studio. Please do with everything as you see fit. I waited until your twenty-fifth birthday to make sure you would grow up with no ties to this life we had in New York. I wanted you to flourish and become the amazing woman I know you to be. This is my last gift to you.

You will also need to meet with Kenneth Williams, my estate attorney, to go over the details of my will and estate.

Please do not fret, my dear one. I know you will have to make some difficult decisions in the next few weeks, but I trust you will do what you think is best.

Just know that I love you and miss you oh so terribly.

- Momma

Calli set the letter aside carefully and slowly slid the Benedettos off. Clutching the shoes to her chest, she let out a low sob.

"I don't want to do this without you, Momma. I really don't!" She stared at the reflection of the shoes in the mirror and cried quietly to herself.

Chapter 2

Being awoken in the middle of the night was not exactly what Calli had planned, but she was certainly awake now. Her heart was racing and she was trembling. She just needed to figure out exactly why she was awake. Looking around her room, she finally set her eyes on the pair of Benedettos she had left at the foot of her bed. Hooking them over the bedpost on the side she was not sleeping on had become second nature.

The stories that had circulated about her the first few years of college when she needed to share a dorm room with someone else had quietly subsided when she was finally able to get a single room. She had done this small ritual with her mother's shoes throughout her life. It gave her the feeling that her mother was with her.

Reaching up with both hands to wipe the sleep from her eyes, she caught a glimpse of the tattoo that stretched across both of her wrists. She had the phrase 'Oh my stars…' in a flowing font and with a smattering of small different-sized stars. 'Oh my' started on her left wrist and 'stars…' finished on the right.

Her mother used to say this at least a dozen times a day, depending on what kind of shenanigans Calli had gotten into. She was not a bad child by any stretch of the imagination, but she was not perfectly behaved one hundred percent of the time either. There was always somewhere to explore, something to see, something to draw on, or flowers to dance through. Calli had been a very active and imaginative child.

She gently traced the tattoo, remembering back to when she got it. Calli had woken up on the day she turned eighteen and could not stop thinking about her mother and the saying. Getting the words tattooed on her seemed like a no-brainer. She went to the only tattoo shop in Clover and explained why and what she wanted.

It was perfect. The tattooist was incredibly nice and patient with her. It had not hurt as much as she had thought it would, but it would definitely be her only one. She thought her mother would approve of the little tattoo, even though her mother never had any herself.

That is what had woken her. She had been dreaming about her mother.

"Oh my stars! Calliope Josephine Morgan! Where on earth have you scampered off to?" her mother called out frantically as she ran up the pathway leading up to the castle. They had decided to take a trip to Central Park to see the Belvedere Castle. Calli had run ahead and was trying to climb up the short wall surrounding the castle grounds so she could see out to the Turtle Pond. She absolutely loved seeing all the different-sized turtles.

"Calliope! Darling, I told you that you needed to stay with me! You impetuous child! Why can't you ever just stay with me?"

Calli only just made it to the first floor of the castle grounds. Her mother stood breathing heavily after finally catching up to where Calli had been trying to climb up the wall. Calli, of course, did not notice that her mother looked sickly and white as a sheet, she was too set on seeing the turtles.

"But, Momma, I want to see the turtles! I wanna count how many there are today!"

Gabriella took a moment to catch her breath. It seemed like she was always trying to catch her breath now. "I know how exciting the turtles are, but you need to make sure to stay with me, okay? I don't want to ever lose you, my sweet."

Calli twirled around to see her mother standing with a hand on her hip. She immediately ran over to her and said, "Oh, Momma, you could never ever lose me." She reached up with both hands and pulled her mother down to her level. After she was crouched down, Calli put her hands on either side of her mother's face. "We will always be together! Forever, right?"

"Yes, darling. Forever and ever. Now let's go see some turtles, shall we?" She stood up slowly and held out her hand. Calli eagerly took it and started to skip ahead as they went to the wall on the side of Turtle Pond.

This was a few months before her mother was admitted to the hospital. Calli still wrestled with the thought of her being so wound up in her own silly day-to-day life while her mother was so sick. And she had barely even noticed.

The guilt was still a heavy burden on her. Some days she was able to not think about it. Most days now, if she was being honest. It had become a part of her normal daily life. But with the appearance of Derrick and the note from her mother, it all came crashing back.

She grabbed the Benedettos and quickly turned on the light next to her on the nightstand. Her hands were shaking as she reached over to grab her reusable water bottle and tried to unscrew the cap. It took her more than a couple tries before she was able to gulp down any of the water.

Pushing the comforter off, she crossed her legs and set the Benedettos on her crossed feet. She closed her eyes and forced herself to take several deep breaths to try and calm down.

The anxiety and panic attacks that she struggled with since her mother's passing had decreased as she had gotten older. Being in control of her life and every aspect of it helped ease the feeling that she was no longer in control.

After a few moments of deep, steady breathing, her shaking stopped and her racing heart returned to normal. She reached over to the nightstand and picked up her mother's letter and the plane ticket.

She traced her mother's handwriting again, somehow hoping she would be able to glean some kind of insight from it. Some way of knowing what the right decision would be.

She did not want to go to New York. Not at all. She was comfortable with her life and daily routine. But she couldn't shake the feeling that she had to go. If only to finalize things so that she would be able to return to her life here in Clover and never have to go to New York City again.

However, she was interested in doing all the touristy things one typically does in New York. Like visiting the Statue of Liberty, Times Square, going to the Metropolitan Museum of Art for all the amazing art, and, of course, Central Park. From what she remembered, she could spend several days at the park and still not see everything.

Calli slipped out of bed and padded over to one of the bookcases nearest her bed to where she kept her extra art supplies. She liked to have backups, just in case. She grabbed one of the smaller sketch pads and a case of her charcoals.

Climbing back into bed, she opened the pad of paper and the charcoals before selecting a piece. She set the charcoal on top of one of the blank pages and closed her eyes. A few moments later, she started sketching.

This was something she had learned in an art class in college. It had helped her art in so many ways that she still frequently did it. She did not have a specific idea in mind, but her hand knew exactly what to draw.

After a short time, she stopped her sketch and opened her eyes. She had drawn a tree peony. In fact, it was the very same tree peony that was pictured in the framed photograph above her bed.

Her mother had gotten the print from a friend she had said. It had been taken in the New York Botanical Gardens shortly before Calli was born. She remembered growing up with it always hanging above her bed. It was one of the reasons the peony was her favorite flower.

Well, that settles it. I suppose I'm going to New York.

Chapter 3

The next morning, Calli made her way down to the flower shop. Her Aunt Maggie may be a little on the eccentric side, but she definitely knows how to arrange a beautiful floral display. Maggie's creativity always blew her away.

After her mother had passed away, Calli was not sure where she would be going. She had thought maybe one of her mother's many friends in New York would try to adopt her, but the week her mother went into the coma, Maggie was there. And she had been there ever since. Calli counts her lucky stars everyday that her Aunt Maggie came into her life when she needed her the most.

Calli stopped at the door frame next to the back room to watch her aunt working. Maggie's outfits never match. Ever. She had initially thought it was an intentional cry for attention, but after living with her for so many years, she realized Aunt Maggie just does not care.

Today, she was wearing her favorite hibiscus muumuu dress. The leaves in the printed dress were alternatively bright purple and green, and the flowers were a gorgeous vivid pink. Her aunt really couldn't care less if it went with her frizzled mop of curly red hair or not.

Calli cleared her throat before stepping into the room and smiled weakly at her aunt. "So... I'm thinking about going to New York."

Her aunt stopped what she was working on and turned to look at her. "I figured you would. You need to go and see what all your mother left for you in New York, and it would be a good idea to meet your father." She smiled at Calli. "Besides, you haven't been to the city since you were a child. Things will be different for you now."

Calli frowned as she sat next to her aunt at the work area and started handing her the various flowers piled in front of them. This was a normal day for the two of them. Calli usually left most of the flower arranging to her aunt while she did the bookkeeping and tending to the general management of the flower shop. They cultivated a very comfortable and friendly environment there, and both worked hard to keep it that way. "That's kind of why I'm so nervous about going back."

"Why? What do you mean, hon?"

"Well, I don't know anyone there, not even my father. And you will be here all by yourself…and I'm not sure how I feel about that."

"I'll be fine!" Maggie made Calli set the flowers down before taking both of her hands in her own and looked directly into her eyes. "You need a little bit of adventure. You've always been here to help me, and I appreciate that, but you need to find your own way. If you go to New York and decide that it's not for you, then definitely come back home! But you never know what will happen if you don't at least try. You may go out there and fall in love with the city. It was way too busy for me. I liked it when I visited, but I knew I had the option to come home, and that's what made it fun for me."

Aunt Maggie tucked a stray hair back into Calli's bun before turning back to the arrangement she was working on. "Besides, you need to go see about that boy. He definitely has a crush on you. I could tell by the way he was looking at you."

Calli's mouth dropped open for a moment before she asked, "Wait, what boy?!"

"The boy that was here yesterday. The one that brought the letters for you. I saw you both sneaking glances at each other. Not at the same time, which is a huge shame of course. I could literally see the sparks flying." She waggled her eyebrows at Calli.

"Oh my gosh…you are ridiculous. He wasn't 'sneaking glances' at me!" Calli would have definitely noticed him staring at her because she had pretty much stared at him the entire time he was in their little shop. She bopped her aunt's hands with the handful of peonies she picked up and smiled. "He was cute though, huh?"

Maggie smiled at Calli and took a couple of the flowers from her for the arrangement. "Oh, yes, he definitely was."

A week later, Calli arrived in New York City. She had enough time to stay and make sure that the wedding they were preparing for went off without a hitch before heading east.

Her father hadn't given her any contact information, so she was not entirely sure how she was going to get to her mother's old apartment. It had been almost fifteen years since she had been in New York City, and she definitely did not remember the address anymore. However, as she walked towards the baggage claim area, in the middle of a group of uniformed drivers holding signs with their charges' names on them, stood a very tall drag queen. She must have been well over six feet tall barefoot, and with the high heels that she had on she was probably pushing closer to seven feet. The drag queen was holding a huge sign that practically screamed Calli's name in pink and red glitter. That combined with the huge bunch of bright pink and red balloons she was holding made her hard to miss.

She was the tallest person Calli had ever seen, literally towering over the people around her. Her long blonde hair ran down her back in thick, luxurious waves, and her makeup was absolutely perfect. She was wearing a light pink sequined dress that covered her long arms but rested halfway down her thighs to reveal her long milk-chocolate legs. Adding to the whole look was a pair of pink Christian Louboutin Daffodile heels embellished with pink crystals that made Calli smile. She had the exact same pair.

The minute she saw Calli, she screamed and ran right up to her. "Calliope Morgan! You get on over here and let me smother you!" With that, she dropped the sign onto the ground, picked Calli up in her toned arms, and started spinning her around as though she weighed nothing.

As they were twirling around, Calli caught the slightest hint of a very sweet yet not overwhelming perfume. The summery fragrance absolutely matched the Amazonian woman as they spun around. It practically smelled pink, and matched perfectly with what she was wearing.

"Oh my! You really do look just like your mother! Just a bit shorter!" she exclaimed as she finally set Calli down.

Calli was slightly dizzy after the sudden spinning around, but she smiled. "Hi! Um… I'm so sorry, but do I know you?"

"Why, child! Don't you remember me? I am your Fairy God Mother!" With that exclamation, she handed Calli the bunch of balloons she was holding and swung her bright pink Hermès Kelly Birkin handbag forward so she could rummage through it. After a brief search, she pulled out a slim silver case embossed with bright pink cherry blossoms. She opened it to reveal a stack of pale-pink business cards. She carefully slipped one of these between her beautifully manicured pink nails and handed it to Calli with an over-the-top bow.

The card read "Fairy God Mother" with each of the words capitalized and marked with a flourish. Underneath was her name, Frances "Aretha" Thierry, with "Aretha" in a larger font size than the rest of her name.

She smiled brightly at Calli as she flicked her card with one of her long fingernails. "See? FGM reporting for duty! Plus, I was your mother's next-door neighbor and best friend, so I'm here to take you to her apartment and make sure you get settled."

"Ah, okay…" Calli was not quite sure what to think of the whole 'I'm your Fairy God Mother' part of her story, but the mention of being her mother's neighbor sparked a memory. There really was no forgetting a six-foot-plus tall person for an eight-year-old. Calli remembered thinking she was some kind of exotic giant or maybe an Amazon. She used to come over and have tea with her mom and always brought Calli a new sketchbook or drawing pencils.

"Now, child, let's go see about your luggage, and then we are off to your mother's apartment!" Aretha smiled and offered Calli her elbow. She could tell the only option she had was to hook her arm through Aretha's while they walked. Calli was positive that Aretha had even started to skip but thought better of it and walked demurely down to baggage claim.

"Here we are!" Aretha exclaimed as they walked through the airport parking lot toward a fantastic pink convertible Cadillac. It looked kind of like a futuristic spaceship, or at least what someone in the early '50s would assume a spaceship would look like.

"Oh, wow! That's a gorgeous car! Do we get to drive with the top down?" Calli pulled The Beast to the trunk of the car and placed her carry-on luggage on top of it. The yellow-and-navy-colored license plate read "ARETHA".

"No! Sorry, doll, but I spent way too long getting this gorgeous hair to do what I wanted it to do and not what *it* wanted to do." Aretha laughed. "But I promise we will take it out for an adventure one day while you are here and we will most definitely have the top down!"

Calli chuckled. She couldn't help it; Aretha's bubbly personality was infectious.

Aretha opened the trunk and helped put her luggage inside. After The Beast was carefully stowed, Aretha unlocked the passenger side door and opened it for Calli. "If you'll hop in, I'll take you to your mother's apartment! I did some remodeling for you, just updating it a bit. I kept your mother's rooms the same, obviously."

She got into the pink Cadillac, and Aretha closed the door softly before walking quickly over to the driver's side and folding her tall frame into the car. As she reached over to grab the seatbelt, her perfume gently wafted toward Calli. It just smelled happy.

"Hey, Aretha, can I ask you a question?" Calli asked.

"Of course, dear! What do you want to know?"

"What perfume are you wearing? I've never smelt something that just fits with a person like yours does! It's kind of magical."

"It's Hanae Mori Eau De Collection No. 4! It actually isn't made anymore unfortunately, so I spent an inordinate amount of time scouring eBay and different websites to find as many bottles as possible. I have quite the hoard at home. I'll have to show you!"

Calli smiled warmly at her. "I know exactly what you mean about hoarding things. I have a certain type of eraser that I like to use when I'm drawing and I'm scared the company will stop making it. So I've bought a bunch just in case!" She chuckled.

"Oh, I almost forgot! Here, I have something for you." Aretha opened up her purse and handed Calli an envelope. She instantly recognized her mother's handwriting.

"Sweet! Thank you, Aretha. I'm excited to read this!" Calli immediately opened it very carefully.

"Now, keep in mind I don't regularly drive in the city, but this car just needs to be seen on occasion. And having you come back was definitely an occasion where I needed to bring this baby out," she said as she reached over to pat Calli's knee. She inserted the key into the ignition, and the engine turned over. The car burst into life with a roar that subsided into a lovely growl.

Calli put on her seatbelt, then pulled the letter from the envelope. When she saw her mother's handwriting again, she smiled brightly. "I'm going to read this now, if that's okay?"

"Sure, dear! Just ignore any screeching or cursing you may hear from me." Aretha chuckled as she backed out of the parking spot. "We are lucky your flight came in now and not during rush hour traffic, so it shouldn't be all too bad getting to the apartment."

"Okay, will do!" Calli smiled again at her Fairy God Mother before turning back to the letter.

It was only a single sheet of paper, but she already knew she would treasure it just like she treasures her mother's shoes and the other letter from her mother that Derrick had given her.

My Dearest Calliope,

I am so very pleased that you decided to return home! I know that my dear friend Aretha will be a great asset to you during this change of pace. She is the most honest and amazing person I have ever met. She will definitely tell you like it is, do not fret about that!

Please let her know if you need anything while you are here. I have left a small trust fund in your name with Aretha, so she will have access to that to cover anything you may possibly need while you are in New York.

Aretha is my dearest friend, and I couldn't have done half the things I accomplished in my life without her. She is amazing. I honestly couldn't tell you how she manages to do all the things she does and still looks absolutely perfect. She really is the best Fairy God Mother a girl could have.

I love you dearly and hope this time in New York goes smoothly for you. I know whatever you decide will make me incredibly proud.

-Momma

Calli wiped a tear from her eye before carefully folding the letter and setting it on the dashboard. She cleared her throat before saying, "Please don't let me forget that letter. My bags are all in the trunk."

"No problem! If you want, you can put it in my purse, although I can't be sure we will be able to find it again. My Birkin has a habit of swallowing things if I'm not careful." She giggled to herself.

Calli realized they were about to drive through Times Square. It was bustling with activity, even in the early afternoon. She did not remember a lot from her childhood in New York, but she did remember Times Square was busy then as well. It had changed in the fifteen years or so since she had been here, but it had the same feeling as when she was a child. Incredibly busy.

"I figured seeing Times Square would be something you would want to do! We will need to come back at night so you can see it all lit up like a crazy Christmas tree. It's like a light bulb store threw up!" She laughed gleefully.

"So, in my mother's letter, she said you are going to help me get everything wrapped up so I can go back to Oregon. Thank you for helping me."

"Oh, don't make a big deal out of it! Of course I would help Gabby's daughter! Why on earth wouldn't I? She's one of the founding members of the original troupe of supermodels, after all."

"Really? How did I not know that about her?"

"Well, she started out with them all—Cindy Crawford, Linda Evangelista, Naomi Campbell, etc. But she got pregnant with you shortly after their rise, so she quietly bowed out of the limelight." Aretha stopped at a light and looked incredulously at her. "Do you not know your mother's history?"

"I know she was a model and was very popular when she was active in the industry, but I haven't ever seen any of her photographs or anything. It's just too painful for me, if that makes sense. I don't want to see her life before me. I know that's selfish, but I like the image I have of her in my head. My sweet mother, not a supermodel, you know?"

"Oh dear, I guess that makes sense. If you ever want to see any of her old photographs or anything, please just let me know. She gave me all her old portfolios, and I have them stored in my apartment."

"Okay, thank you, Aretha." She smiled while she took in her surroundings. They had pulled up to a large apartment complex, and Aretha was currently punching in the code for the gated parking garage.

"Is this where my mother's apartment is?"

"Yes! And I'm directly across the hall from you, so if you need anything, all you need to do is ask." Aretha pulled into a parking spot near the elevator, turned off the Cadillac, and grabbed her Birkin. "Now, let's get upstairs so we can get you settled!"

Chapter 4

"You do know that you are going to have to show me what all you've got in your mother's shoe trunk, right?" Aretha looked at her expectantly as she fumbled in her purse for the keys to Calli's mother's apartment. "Aha! There they are!" she exclaimed as she pulled out a key on a shiny silver Tiffany's keyring with a large silver star charm.

"Sure, I'll show you my shoes, but don't be surprised if you don't ever see me wearing them around. They are 'look and see' only."

Aretha arched her perfectly plucked eyebrows. "Look and see, huh?" With a flourish, she opened the door and stepped into the apartment. "Interesting."

"Yep! Most of them were my mom's, so I don't wear them out of the house."

Calli took a deep breath before stepping into the apartment she had shared with her mother all those years ago. The front door opened up into a large entryway with a small ornate table to the left.

She paused for a moment by the little table remembering the last time she had seen it. It was the day her aunt packed up Calli's room and took her and everything she owned back to Oregon.

Aretha handed her the apartment key. "But you wear your shoes out, right?"

"Um…no, they stay in the case with the rest of the shoes." Calli distractedly put the key into her pants pocket as she wandered further into the apartment.

From the entryway, the apartment opened up to a large room that acted as both the living room and kitchen. The furniture had all been updated by Aretha, but it still had the same open feeling as it had before.

Calli rolled the shoe trunk up behind the low white couch and tossed her carry-on luggage on top of it.

On the right-hand side of the room were the doors to the bedrooms. She did not bother going into her old room but went straight into her mother's room. It was exactly as she remembered it.

It opened up to a large king-size four-poster bed in the center of the room against the main wall. To the right was her mother's desk, and to the left was her mother's makeup table. There was also a large side door on the left that opened up to the huge walk-in closet and bathroom.

Calli headed directly into the closet. She picked up the first article of clothing there, a black-and-white Chanel dress, and held it under her nose. Somehow, it still smelled of her mother. "Chanel N°5," she murmured softly to herself.

Aretha cleared her throat from the doorway a moment later. "You know they are all yours now, right?"

"What is?" asked Calli, straightening the dress on the hanger and setting it back with the rest of the clothes.

"All your mother's clothes." Aretha gestured to the closet. "Everything here in the apartment."

"Oh. Well, I don't want it. Any of it. We can donate it to charity or something."

Aretha looked at her incredulously. "You don't want any of your mother's clothes?"

"No. I have no use for them. Her shoes are enough."

Aretha threw up her hands. "You are out of your mind! Those shoes were made to be worn, not sit in that chest like some obscure museum! You've never worn them outside? Ever?"

"Nope, I just wear my good old clogs."

Aretha looked like she had a terrible taste in her mouth and pursed her lips. "Hmm, well let me see those clogs. Maybe they aren't as bad as I think they are."

Calli slipped off her clogs and handed them over to Aretha. She was acting a little strange.

"So, are these the only pair you've brought along with you?"

"Yes, I only brought this pair. Why would I need to bring any others? I won't be here for very long."

"Great!" Aretha took the clogs carefully by the heels and made a beeline for the nearest window. She carried them out in front of her like they were something deeply horrendous.

"Wait! What are you doing?!"

"Darling, these 'shoes' are downright dreadful! They need to be set free!" And with that statement, she opened the window and tossed them out.

"Those are my only pair of shoes! What are you thinking?!" Calli ran to the open window and gazed down the thirty stories to the ground below. Luckily, there was not anyone walking on the sidewalk below otherwise they would have a lot of explaining to do. "You know those aren't cheap! Those are Danskos! They're like over a hundred bucks!"

Calli turned to see Aretha going through her luggage. "What do you think you are doing?" Calli put her hands on her hips and frowned at her supposed Fairy God Mother.

"Checking out your clothes to see if they are as dreadfully boring as what you are currently wearing." She sighed dramatically and shook her head. "Just as I thought!" Aretha gathered up the few pairs of pants and shirts Calli brought into her arms and stealthily stalked back toward the window.

"Now, child, you are going to need to move. I need to set these terrible clothes free as well!"

Calli stood her ground, crossing her arms over her chest. "No! Definitely not! I won't have anything to wear! And I made those!"

Aretha paused with a shocked look on her face, tossed the clothes over one shoulder, and held up one of the pairs of pants to inspect them. "Hmmm... I mean, they could possibly have some potential, but the coloring is WAY off. Way too boring!" She shrugged and put them with the rest of the clothes on her shoulder. "You know you are going to have to move, right? You're all of what...five feet, six...maybe seven inches? And you don't weigh more than a hundred and twenty pounds. There isn't any way you are going to be able to stop me, dear. So just get out of my way and let me do what needs to be done!"

Calli threw up her arms in disgust. "Oh my gosh! You've lost your mind! I can't go anywhere without any shoes! And I can't very well wear this same exact outfit every day I am here! What on earth is WRONG with you?!"

Aretha threw the armful of clothes out the window before shutting it softly. "Now, dear child, I know this may come as a bit of a shock to you, but I can't have you walking around this town looking like some unadventurous college student. You are your mother's daughter, and now it's time for you to look the part! You've got a case full of beautiful shoes right there that you can wear." She gestured to The Beast with a smile. "And you now have access to your mother's closet! Some of it may be a little bit outdated, but I know we can find plenty of outfits for you to wear."

Calli sat down on the couch and scowled. "There was nothing at all wrong with my clothes! It took me a very long time to get those pants to fit just right. I can't believe I just let you do that!"

"Oh, honey, please don't take it personally. If you want, we can go out to the fabric shops in the fashion district and you can make yourself some new pants. But until then, we need to go see what we can find in that closet of yours." She went over and grabbed Calli's hands, pulling her up from the couch.

"This is gonna get serious, so I'd better prepare!" Aretha smiled and pulled off the heels she was wearing, carefully setting them on the coffee table. "Now, I can't be running around your mother's closet in those all night! My poor feet would run away accusing me of abuse!" She chuckled to herself as she pulled Calli to the closet.

Aretha pulled out the chair in front of her mother's makeup table and placed it in the doorway to the closet. Turning on the overhead light, she gestured eagerly for Calli to sit down. "Might as well get comfortable, dear, we are going to be here for a little while! But I'll take you out to dinner as soon as we are all done. I promise." She smiled sweetly at Calli and patted the seat.

Calli continued to scowl but sat on the stool as requested. "I don't know if any of these clothes are going to fit me. My mom was so much taller than I am."

Aretha mock-scowled back at her for a moment before turning to look at the clothes hanging in the closet. "Now, honey, your momma was only five-foot-ten. You aren't that much shorter than her. And with your sewing skills, I'm sure you can hem anything that might be too long."

Calli rolled her eyes and stuck out her tongue at Aretha's back.

"You keep that tongue where it belongs, missy, or it'll be joining your beloved clogs out on the sidewalk." Aretha gave her a pointed look over her shoulder. "Don't you sass me."

"Sorry…" Calli mumbled, wondering how the heck she knew she was sticking her tongue out at her if Aretha's back was turned.

"Now, stop pouting and come try on this little dress." She held up the Chanel dress that Calli had grabbed earlier and looked skeptically back and forth between her and the dress.

"Ok…" Calli got up and took the dress from Aretha, then retreated into the bathroom.

"We are also going to have to do something about that hair of yours," Aretha called out to her as she changed. Calli glared at the door and stomped her feet. What on earth was wrong with her hair? She kept it tamed and secure in her bun, there was no way she was going to let it be as frizzy and out of control as her aunt's hair. Calli was all about control.

Calli could hear Aretha talking to someone outside the door and hurried to finish getting dressed.

"Who were you talking to?" Calli asked as she stepped out of the bathroom, looking around the room skeptically.

"Oh, I was just getting one of my friends to come over and see about that hair of yours," Aretha explained. Calli did not see a phone in her hand and was about to ask how she had talked to her friend, but Aretha plowed on. "Here! Let me zip you up!"

Aretha grabbed her by the shoulders and spun her around so she could get to the zipper. As she reached down to straighten the dress before zipping her up, Calli could have sworn the dress shrank at least two inches, but it could have been how it rested on her body without the zipper being fully closed. "Oh my gosh! See! It fits you perfectly, dear!"

Calli sighed quietly. Aretha was right, the dress did fit her exactly as it should. It was a sleeveless black shift dress that rested just above Calli's knees. The top was a keyhole scoop neck that had six strips of white piping running in a lovely crisscross pattern across it. It was absolutely stunning.

"Now, let's go see about a pair of shoes, shall we? I want to see what all you've got hidden away in that massive trunk of yours." Aretha clapped her hands excitedly and pushed Calli gently out of the room. "You better have your mother's Benedettos in there or we are going to have a HUGE problem."

Calli laughed. "Oh, yes! I definitely have her Benedettos. They're my favorite pair!"

Calli swung the trunk around so that she could open it. "Now, most of these are my mother's, but I added the ones on the bottom. Which pair do you want to see? The Benedettos?"

"Oh, child, just let me at them! I'm like a kid in a candy store! Oh my goodness!" Aretha exclaimed, "You've got the same pair of Louboutins as I do!"

Calli smiled as Aretha pulled out the box with her sparkly pink Louboutins in it. "Yeah, I know. They're one of my favorite pairs. They're very princess-like to me."

Just then someone rang the doorbell. "Who on earth could that be? How does anyone even know that I am here?"

"Oh, that's one of my coworkers and my best friend. He's here to fix that plain-Jane hair of yours," Aretha said from the floor. "We can't have you going out looking like some old-school marm while you are here. You need to look absolutely FAB-U-LOUS!" Aretha smiled up at her. "At least you have the shoes covered! Go ahead and get the door, darling." Aretha half-heartedly shooed her, but as soon as Calli started toward the front door, her attention went back to the bounty of shoes in front of her.

Calli opened the front door to an impeccably dressed man. He had on one of the best cut-off white suits she had ever seen; it fit him absolutely perfectly, like a second skin. Even without a tie, he looked very dashing. What was left of his grey hair was buzzed very short behind his ears. Across his chin, he had a sprinkling of salt-and-pepper-colored stubble. One hand was resting on his hip while the other was resting nonchalantly on a pull handle for the large black rolling case next to him. He cleared his throat and looked Calli up and down. "Well, now I see what all the fuss is about."

"What?! Oh gosh, I don't think I look that bad." Calli frowned at him.

"Oh, you don't look bad per se. You look just positively...boring. You would definitely get lost in the crowds if you went out into the city by yourself." He arched one of his perfectly shaped brows at her. "So, are you going to let me in, or am I going to stand out here all night?"

Calli blushed and stepped out of his way. "Oh gosh... Yes, please do come inside."

She led the way back into the living room where Aretha was now fully surrounded by all of the shoes. Aretha was holding the pair of

Benedettos with a look of pure rapture on her face. "These are so amazingly gorgeous! Honey child, you are SO lucky we aren't even close to having the same shoe size or these would go a-missing."

Aretha got up quickly from the floor and handed Calli the Benedettos. "Here, you have to wear these shoes with that dress. It's like they are in sync. Definitely meant to be together. I bet even your mother wore them together." Aretha smiled mischievously at Calli. "Now, dear, let's see what Fairy Gary can do for you!"

Calli followed Aretha back into her mother's bedroom where Gary—she refused to call him fairy anything—had started to unpack his case onto the makeup table. There were all kinds of tubes and containers of makeup and other miscellaneous beauty products, as well as every conceivable piece of hair equipment. He was definitely a professional.

"Sit, please." Gary gestured to the chair he had pulled back into place. Calli quietly obliged. "First, we are going to see what we can do about this hair of yours, then we will move on to makeup. I assume you aren't wearing anything, am I correct?" He asked Calli with a mock scowl. She could tell he was actually kind of enjoying himself though.

"Nope. Nothing. I don't see the point really, to be honest."

"Oh my goodness me. Well, we will make sure you have a moment of clarity, dear. After today, I bet you twenty bucks you will never leave the house without at least a bit of concealer, powder, and some lip gloss on."

Calli smiled. "Oh, I'll take you up on that."

"I am going to be looking through the rest of this treasure trove of a closet while Fairy Gary works his magic on you. Holler at me when you two are done!"

Calli waited until her FGM was completely distracted by all the clothes and other miscellaneous items in the closet before she asked quietly, "Why does she call you Fairy Gary?"

Gary looked at her in the mirror and smiled slyly. "Oh, we work together, dear. It's purely a term of endearment." He took a slim black leather business card holder out of his jacket pocket, removed one of the business cards, and handed it to her. Then, he went back to undoing the bun her hair was in.

Calli took the card and looked at it. His was a crisp white card and said "Fairy God Mother" same as Aretha's, but where hers had a flourish with the beginning of each word, his was just simply bold and to the point with his name, Gary Poratti.

"Ah, so you are a Fairy God Mother too then? I didn't realize there was such a calling for them."

"Oh, dear, you don't even know the half of it!" Gary smiled at her and ran his hands through her hair. "Luckily, we won't have to do too much with your hair. Just need to trim the ends and give it a bit of shape but it actually isn't too bad. Why do you always wear it in a bun?"

Calli paused a moment before answering. "It's just easier." She shrugged. "If I ever leave it down, it gets pretty frizzy because of the curls. Especially if there's any humidity in the air, then all bets are completely off as to what it's going to do. Living in Oregon, it's pretty much always humid, so this is the easiest and most efficient way of dealing with my hair."

Gary rested his hands on her shoulders and said, "Well, I have a magic potion that will solve that problem!" He smiled and produced a small bottle of clear liquid. "You put this in your hair right after you are done with your shower and the frizz will be gone. I promise!"

Calli did not necessarily believe him, but she would give it a shot. She was actually starting to get excited about her potential new look.

Gary chatted with her as he trimmed her hair, asking about her life and where she grew up. He never once mentioned her mother or asked why she was in New York. She could feel herself relaxing and became more comfortable as she answered his questions. Whatever he asked, she found herself answering without any qualms.

After an hour or so of his pampering and informative instructions for replicating the hair and makeup, he declared his work was done. He handed Calli the pair of Benedettos and, after she put them on, he led her back into the bathroom with her eyes closed. "Now wait here, I have to go get Aretha. I think she may have gotten lost." She heard him chuckle softly before walking away.

The minute she was sure he was gone, she opened up her eyes.

"Oh, wow..." she murmured softly. He really had worked some kind of magic. Her normally wild and unmanageable red hair was now curled softly in loose spirals around her shoulders, the tips resting just below her collarbone. He had even added bangs that swept delicately to the left side of her face, framing her green eyes. And those eyes! Her normally plain green eyes stood out with the mauve-colored eye shadow he had applied. She had always shied away from red-tinted eye shadows because of her hair, but he explained that with her green eyes the right shade of red or pink would make her eyes POP.

Gary had applied a soft, shimmery peach blush over her cheekbones. He claimed it was his favorite color ever called "Orgasm" by NARS. It created a soft warm glow over her cheekbones. On her lips, he had applied a lip gloss called "Sugar Rose" by Fresh, and outlined her lips with a nude lip liner. He had enhanced each one of her features without making it look like she had applied any makeup at all.

"Oh, Gary...I think she likes it!" Aretha clapped happily, "Look! I think you've got her hooked."

Calli beamed and rushed to hug them both. "Thank you! I really don't know what else to say..." For the first time in her life, Calli could actually say she looked just like her mother. She opted not to say anything about the similarities, but she could tell by the looks on their faces that they saw it too.

Chapter 5

Calli awoke the next morning to someone knocking on the front door. She and the FGMs had decided to just order some Chinese food rather than go out to a restaurant. They were having way too much fun going through her mother's clothes together.

"Hold on a second, jeez!" she called out to whomever was making the racket at the door. Besides the fact that she was still on Oregon time, they had all stayed up until at least two in the morning going through all her mother's clothes. It was just now eight o'clock.

She scrambled to the door and opened it in a huff. "What?!"

Standing at her front door was not Aretha as she had expected, but Derrick.

"Hello there! Good morning." He said with a smirk. She could tell he was trying really hard not to laugh.

"Oh crap. I mean hi. Come in. Let me go get some pants on… Crap." Calli left the front door open and darted back into the bedroom, skidding around the corner because of her socks. She currently had on the extra-large "I Love New York" shirt the Chinese food delivery guy had picked up for her on the way to deliver the food they ordered. Her comfy pajama pants and t-shirt had gotten tossed out with the rest of her clothes. Other than the giant t-shirt and her boy-short underwear, she was completely bare.

"I take it your father forgot to tell you that I was coming over this morning to take you to see the estate lawyer?" he called out to her. "Or that you are supposed to go have dinner with him tonight?"

"Um…no. I haven't talked to my father. Ever, actually," she called back from the bedroom.

"It's alright. I'm glad I came over early now."

She found the clothes she had worn on the plane on the other side of the bed, so she tossed on the black slacks and light grey shirt. Luckily, her hair was behaving and was not in a huge rats' nest at the back of her head like it normally was when she woke up. "So, what time am I supposed to meet with Kenneth? That was his name right?" she asked as she walked back into the living room.

"Yes, Kenneth Williams. We are scheduled to meet him at ten o'clock." He cleared his throat and handed her a medium-sized black box with a stylistic white 'S' on top of it. "Here, this was left outside your front door when I came up."

"Thanks." She took the box and read the card tied to the top of it.

This should get you through the day until you and I can go shopping at Sephora.

- *Gary*

Smiling, she opened up the box to find all the makeup products he had used on her the night before. There was even a complete set of full-sized makeup brushes included, so she was good to go to recreate the look from last night. She was not sure how Gary had been able to gather everything so quickly. Maybe he had a pile of backup supplies that he gave out to his clients or something always on-hand. However it was that he had been able to get everything, she was very thankful to him and would make sure he knew that.

She tugged at her shirt self-consciously. "Does this look okay? Or should I change into something else?"

He furrowed his brows at her. "What do you mean?"

"I'm just wondering if you think it looks okay or if I should go get something from my mother's closet." She bit her lip softly.

"Well, I think you look fine. Besides, you are just going to meet your mother's lawyer. It's not like we are going anywhere fancy or anything like that."

"Okay, give me a minute to brush my teeth and stuff, then we will get going."

"Sure, no problem." He plopped down onto one of the white couches, eyeing the mess of shoes scattered all over the living room floor.

"My FGM— I mean, my mother's neighbor picked me up from the airport and we ended up having a girls' night last night. Which means she mainly spent all night drooling all over my shoes. Sorry about the mess."

"It's okay, no worries," he replied.

"I'll be right back." She grabbed the box of makeup goodies from Gary and ran into the bathroom.

Minutes later, she heard him shuffling around in the kitchen.

"I think there's a coffee maker in there somewhere. I can't remember," she called out to him.

"Yeah, I found it. Would you like one?"

"No, thank you. I only really drink tea if I'm having caffeine. If there's any green tea in there, I'd happily take one, but I don't think I saw a teapot."

She heard him chuckle but did not get any other response. Shrugging, she went back to trying to recreate the makeup application she had learned last night. It was a little bit more difficult than she thought it would be. Putting on the eyeshadow and the blush was alright, but the mascara? Now that was scary! After a couple of mess-ups, she ended up having to completely redo her right eye because she smeared mascara all over her eyelid. She finally figured it was as good as it was going to get. Working with pencils and chalks on paper was completely different than trying to paint her face.

"Sorry about that," she told Derrick as she walked back out into the living room. He was lounging on the couch with his phone in his hand, sipping a cup of coffee.

"It's okay, we've got plenty of time to get to Kenneth's, so no worries." He put his phone back in his pocket, then handed her the coffee mug that was sitting on the coffee table with a smile. "Here's your tea."

"Thanks! I'm glad you found tea bags."

"Oh, there's no teapot or tea bags. I just used the single-serve coffee maker you have."

"How does a coffee maker make tea? I mean I know you could just not put any coffee in the filter and use the hot water, but where's the tea bag?" She sipped from the mug he had offered her, it actually tasted pretty good. Just needed to add a touch of honey.

"Here, I'll show you." He went over into the kitchen to an oddly shaped machine. It looked a bit like a regular old coffee maker, but it didn't have the part where you would put the filter or the coffee grounds.

He gestured to the carousel that held a bunch of little pods. Grabbing one, he reached over and opened the front of the coffee machine and put in the tiny container. He closed it, put his now empty mug under the spigot, then pushed a button on the top. A few seconds later, a hot stream of coffee poured into the cup.

"You can pick whatever flavor you want, see?" He slowly spun the carousel that held a variety of different little containers. From different flavors of tea and coffee to even hot chocolate. He opened up the arm where he had placed the pod and removed the now used container and tossed it into the trash. "I LOVE these things. Seriously, the greatest invention ever. I can't believe you guys don't have one of these back home." He took a drink from the new cup of coffee he had just made to show her how much he loved it.

"Naw, my aunt is a hardcore tea drinker like me. We've got quite the collection of tea kettles. Some are even antiques."

"So, are you ready to go?" he asked as he dumped what was left of his coffee into the sink and quickly cleaned his cup. "We should get going because you never know what the traffic is going to be like. Generally, it's just pretty bad."

"Yep, let me just grab some shoes and my wallet, then we can go."

"Just a wallet huh? No purse or anything?" He looked at her quizzically again. She was beginning to wonder if this was his default expression.

She went over to where her shoes were scattered all over the floor and picked up one of the pairs of Ferragamo Vara pumps. They had the smallest heel in her collection by far, only one and a half inches, and they would do nicely as an everyday shoe. She absolutely loved the little grosgrain bow on the top. In fact, she adored these little heels so much that she had gotten two new pairs of the black version. One with silver hardware and one with brass. She slipped the silver accented pair on her feet before heading toward the door.

Pausing by the little ornate table next to the door, she grabbed the silver antique cigarette case and the star keychain Aretha had given her with the apartment key on it. She turned towards Derrick and showed him the little case. "See? I don't have a purse or anything. Just this little old case my mom had, even though she never smoked. I use it for my wallet."

"Interesting. Okay, well let's get going." He walked to the front door and held it open for her. She tried to ignore the little flutter she felt in her stomach when she walked by him, but it was really hard not to.

"So tell me, how are you liking New York so far?" Kenneth Williams asked in a crisp British accent as they sat down in his office. He sat behind a massive dark cherry desk and she sat in one of the two chairs in front of the desk. Calli had been expecting a tiny doddering old man but Kenneth had surprised her. Yet another incredibly tall person to add to her new world. He was probably as tall as Aretha, minus the high heels of course. Although he was impeccably dressed, none of his clothing necessarily matched. He had on a black pin-striped suit, a bright blue plaid shirt, and a teal paisley bow tie.

"Well, it's been interesting so far. I just arrived in the city last night so I haven't really seen a lot of New York yet. The car ride here was fun though. I'm amazed by all the different shops. And all the people! Holy smokes, it's kinda crazy."

"Yes, it's definitely a change for almost anyone when they come here, and I'm sure things have changed dramatically since you were last here. It's been, what? Fifteen years or so?"

"Yeah, it'll be eighteen years in February. That's when she passed away."

"Your mother was actually one of my very first clients. She was such a lovely woman."

"Thank you. I miss her every day." Calli cleared her throat softly and adjusted in the chair before meeting his eyes. "So, you need to go over her estate or whatever with me, right?"

"I do. Your mother was actually very smart about her money—well, your money now—and had me put most of the funds into various investment accounts. She also had me set up a trust fund for you, which you'll have access to on your twenty-fifth birthday." He smiled as Calli nodded. "Basically, what I need to know is what you would like me to do with the different funds your mother invested in. Should I cash them out now or leave them so that they accrue more interest?"

"Well I don't have any student loans or anything. I was able to get scholarships and grants for that, so I'm good there. And my aunt already owns her house and the flower shop, so she's pretty much set as far as that goes. I guess whatever is left, just let it sit and build interest?"

"Sounds like a plan. I will just leave them be, to earn more interest. And don't worry about your aunt, your mother had a separate account set up that has been sending payments to her since your she passed away. I will make sure you have access to your trust fund account as well. Your birthday is September eighteenth, correct?"

"Correct. I will be twenty-five."

"Well, happy early birthday to you." He chuckled softly. "We will have to make sure you have a great day that day."

"Thank you. I was thinking I would be back in Oregon by then so we will see."

"I will try to get everything set up so you won't have to stay here any longer than you wanted. What did you want to do with your mother's apartments? Those are in your name currently and are completely paid off. Would you prefer to keep them or would you like me to contact a realtor and sell them once your time here comes to a close?"

"Well, I guess we can sell them once I go back to Oregon. Although, I don't know what you are talking about with the plural 'apartments'. There's only one that I'm staying in right now."

"Hmm, I could have sworn your mother had two different apartments, and I thought they were in the same building. I'm sorry, I should have had all the paperwork here for our meeting today. I anticipated you would know what I was talking about. I apologize."

"Oh no! It's okay! If there is another apartment, we will definitely sell that one seeing as I'm not using it right now."

"Okay, I will look into that and give you a call by tomorrow night at the latest. Do you have a cell phone number where I can reach you?"

Calli cleared her throat. "No, actually, I don't have a cell phone. My aunt and I generally stay at home or in the town we live in and haven't really ever had the need for one. And I have no idea what the number is for my mother's apartment, or if it even has a phone. If you'll give me your business card, I will give you a call tomorrow, say at three o'clock?" She did not understand what everyone's infatuation with being connected and reachable all the time was. She could not wait until she was able to get everything done here and go back home.

"Of course. I'll also write my home number on the back just in case you need to reach me outside of office hours. I'll be available." He scribbled on the back of his card before handing it to her. She was half expecting to see "Fairy God Mother" typed under his name, but this card just held his name, title, and phone number. Calli smiled and put it in her wallet with the other business cards she had collected since arriving in New York.

"Is there anything else? I believe I'm going to have an early dinner with my father tonight and would like to go get ready."

"No, that's all for now. I will speak to you tomorrow about the apartments. Have a good day and enjoy dinner with your father." Kenneth stood up from his chair and came around the desk to envelop her in a hug. "I am very happy you are here at last to finalize your mother's estate. I do hope that you find your trip to New York agreeable and choose to stay with us a little bit longer."

She smiled and returned the hug. "Thank you. I will talk to you tomorrow."

"What time am I supposed to have dinner with my father again?" Calli asked Derrick on the ride back to the apartment. Her father hired a private car for her to use while she was in New York, so she and Derrick were sitting in the back together. "I'm sorry, I know you said the time earlier today, but I've completely forgotten."

"Dinner will be at six o'clock at a great Italian restaurant by Gramercy Park called Lucca. They've got an amazing menu. The owner works closely with local farmers to make sure they have the freshest and highest quality ingredients. I've never eaten there myself, but I've heard wonderful things about it." He said all of this without looking up from his phone. She was beginning to think he had a cell phone addiction.

"What are you doing on that phone that is so important anyway?"

"I'm just checking my Facebook, and having a conversation with someone on Twitter about Roland Arsenault."

"Roland who?"

This statement caused him to actually look up from his phone. "Roland Arsenault. You know, probably one of THE most important photographers in the history of American Fashion? Or just photography in general? He's legendary. I think he even worked with your mother on a few photoshoots. In fact, I'm almost certain he did."

"I guess I will have to look him up then."

"You should, he's amazing. He was actually a fairly good friend of your father's before he passed away."

"How did my father know him, do you know? Did he meet him through my mother or something?"

Derrick put his phone down on the seat and gave her an incredulous look. "Do you not know anything about your father?"

"No, actually, I don't. I mean, I just found out he even existed a few days ago."

"You didn't try looking him up on the internet or anything?"

"Um, no. I guess I could've, but we were so busy trying to get everything set up for that wedding. We had to get all the flower arrangements ready for that. I honestly didn't have time." She frowned at him, "So what, is he like famous too or something?"

"No, not famous like your mother was, but he's definitely well known. He's a photographer, but unlike Roland Arsenault, he is known for his photojournalism. He worked primarily overseas documenting the different wars going on for *The New York Times*. Now he's semi-retired and shoots editorials for various magazines and newspapers." Derrick shook his head. "I don't understand how you don't know any of this. It's all readily available on the internet."

Calli sighed and said, "I know it's weird for you, but back in Clover, there was no need for a phone or the internet really. It was the same thing day in and day out. Go to work at the flower shop, hang out with my aunt, draw or sketch." She shrugged.

"I guess there's a difference between where you live versus where I live. I would be lost without my phone here. I use it for everything."

"I could see how having a cell phone here in New York would be important, but I just don't need one back home."

"I'll try to stay off of it while you're here in town. How about that?"

"Sure, if you want." She found herself smiling at him, and he smiled back. Thankfully, they pulled up to her apartment building before anything got too awkward between them.

"Child! Where on earth have you been?! I've been sitting here all morning worrying about you and wondering where you have gone! Don't you ever leave without at least telling me first! I need your cell phone number so I can make sure you aren't dead in a ditch somewhere or washed out to sea via the Hudson." Aretha was standing next to the open door of her apartment; across the hall, her patent leather pink Yves Saint Laurent heels tapping indignantly on the carpet.

Aretha looked amazing, yet again. Today she had on a short asymmetrical draped Grecian-style dress that made sure to show off her toned arms as well as her muscular legs. Her hair was in a bubbly blonde afro on top of her head that looked more like cotton candy than hair. The dress and hair were the same shade of very light pink.

Calli sighed as she unlocked the door to her mother's apartment. "I don't have a cell phone, Aretha."

"What? Why ever not?" She actually stamped her feet before she walked across the hall to where Calli held open the door for her.

"Because I don't need one back home." She sighed again. "I'm sorry I didn't tell you I was leaving, but it was ridiculously early this morning when Derrick showed up. I just assumed you were still asleep. I had to go to a meeting with the estate lawyer."

Aretha made her way into the apartment, making sure Calli knew how upset she was about being left out by clicking her heels and throwing herself onto the couch with an exaggerated huff. Scowling up at Calli, she crossed her arms over her chest and said, "Well, we will have to fix that problem as soon as possible. At the very least while you are in town, you will need to have some way for me to get ahold of you. I was going to take you to Sephora to go shopping with Gary, but we will have to go tomorrow because he is working right now."

"I am really sorry. I promise to let you know if I'm leaving again. I have dinner with my father at six, but other than that I don't have any plans."

Calli went into the kitchen and selected a black tea container for the little coffee maker. "Do you want a coffee or tea or anything? I'm kinda falling in love with this little coffee maker."

"Oh no, honey, I'm okay." She demurely crossed her legs and put her hands in her lap before continuing, "So, tell me all that the lawyer said, and who is this Derrick person?" Her attention was solely on Calli.

"It went well, I guess. Pretty normal I would expect, but I honestly have no idea how these things go. I'm going to cash out some of my mom's investment accounts so I can pay off my student loans completely. Then Kenneth is going to set up the sale of the apartment after I'm done here." She paused, clearing her throat before continuing. "It was kinda weird though, he mentioned that my mom had a second apartment. Do you know anything about that?"

Aretha frowned. "A second apartment? No, I only know about this one. Maybe she has it set up in another building? That could be a possibility."

"Yeah. I'm supposed to call him tomorrow after he's had a chance to look into it. Do I have a landline here?" She sipped her tea and looked around the living room until she spotted a phone on one of the little end tables. "Never mind. I see it."

Aretha nodded, looking at her expectantly.

"What?!" Calli asked, confused.

Aretha cleared her throat and patted the spot next to her on the couch. "So, tell me, who's this Derrick fellow?" she asked, uncrossing and recrossing her long legs.

"He's my father's assistant. He came out to Oregon to give me the tickets to fly here, and he took me to go see Kenneth this morning. He's been a huge help actually. And he showed me how to use the coffee maker, so that's awesome."

"Mhmmm…I see. Fascinating. So, is he going to dinner with you and your father tonight too?"

"Oh no, it's just going to be me and my father tonight. That should be really interesting." She was not really looking forward to dinner with her father, but she needed to go. If only so she could meet him and then be done with it. It is not like he had ever shown any interest in her life thus far.

Aretha reached over and patted Calli's hand but did not say anything.

"So we can meet up with Gary tomorrow, right? I think going shopping with the two of you will be fun."

"Yes, ma'am! I will get it all set up with him." Aretha sat back and looked at Calli. "You are going to wear the Chanel dress tonight, right? That is definitely your dress, you know."

"That's what I was thinking. The only thing I'm worried about is I won't have anywhere to put my wallet. I usually only wear pants. So it's not like I can stick it in my pocket or anything."

"What are you talking about?"

"I don't actually own any purses really."

"What?! Are you serious?" Aretha pursed her lips. "You mean to tell me you don't own a purse? Of any kind?"

"Nope. I just have my wallet. See?" She pulled the cigarette case out of her back pocket and handed it to Aretha.

Aretha took it, the shocked expression returning to her features. She opened the little case and saw that Calli had a couple of twenty dollar bills, her driver's license, debit card, and the three business cards she'd collected so far. She snapped it closed and tossed it back to Calli.

"Come with me." Aretha got up off the couch and marched into her mother's room.

Calli sighed softly and followed her a moment later.

"You know, you are lucky to have me and this wonderful assortment of goodies from your mother. I shudder to think of how this whole situation would be going otherwise," Aretha called to her from her mother's closet.

When Calli had caught up with her, she was in the back corner of the closet where there were several shelves that held various colored boxes with a range of items from different designers—from Chanel to Louis Vuitton to Hermès.

Aretha looked over to her, smiling from ear to ear. "Welcome to the Holy Grail of purse collections. It may not be as large as some of the other collections out there in the world, but each and every one is special. I swear your mother had the best taste ever in the history of purse collectors. You should keep all of these and never, ever sell them. Or if you do decide to sell them, let me know because I will buy every single one."

"Now tonight, since you are going to be wearing the Chanel dress to dinner, I highly suggest you wear one of the classic mini flap bags by

Chanel. I would wear a splash of color myself, but I believe your mom has a black one in here somewhere."

She went over to the stack of smaller black boxes and pulled one out. 'Chanel' was written on the top of the box in white. "It might take a bit of time finding the black one because your mother had a serious Chanel addiction. I think she has one of every color this size purse came in! The 2.55 Chanel flap is still super popular even today." Aretha giggled and opened the box.

Nestled in the tissue paper stamped with the two interlocking 'C's of the Chanel logo laid the most adorable red quilted leather purse. Aretha laughed, "Of course she would have this one on the top. Red was her favorite color after all." She handed it over to Calli before she took another box from the stack.

"Really? I didn't know that. I guess I never thought about what her favorite color was. I just assumed she loved them all." Calli smiled as she looked at the little purse. "Red is my favorite color too."

"Ah! Here we are!" Aretha opened the next box and traded it with the box Calli was holding. Inside was the same purse but in black. "What do you think?"

Calli gingerly took the purse out of the tissue and set the empty box on top of the other boxes on the shelf. It was made from the softest leather Calli had ever felt and she sighed happily as she ran her hands over the quilted flap before opening it. The purse had a second flap that covered the inside compartment and it was made of the same soft leather as the outside, just not quilted. She would doubtlessly have enough room for her small cigarette case. She even loved the bit of black leather that was woven into the silver chain of the strap.

She looked up from the purse to see Aretha watching her expectantly. "Oh, this will be just perfect I think." Calli traced the small interlocking silver 'C's by the clasp with a wistful smile on her lips.

"Ooh, girl! You are definitely hooked now. I can see that Chanel smile!" Aretha clapped her hands gleefully. "Now, let's see what other gorgeous pieces your mother stashed in here...."

Calli carefully set the purse back in its box and placed it on the island inside the closet. "It's almost like Christmas, isn't it?" she asked her FGM.

Aretha smiled and tossed her arm around Calli's shoulders. "Oh, it definitely is!"

Chapter 6

Quietly drumming her fingers on the crisp white tablecloth, Calli wondered how much longer her father would be. She looked over at the large farmhouse-style clock that was on one of the walls near her table. He was officially fifteen minutes late. Way to make a great first impression, Dad. She sighed and looked out across the restaurant.

Lucca was an Italian restaurant and bar, and it was incredibly charming. She felt quite at ease even though she was finally meeting the man partially responsible for her existence. She was surprised she felt as comfortable as she did. The white tablecloth was neatly arranged over a blue and white checkered cloth. The restaurant had a quaint old Italian home feel to it with the exposed wooden beams in the ceiling.

The VIP section that she was seated in was next to where they stored stacks and stacks of amazing-looking bread, various blocks of cheese, and other miscellaneous dessert items like cookies and muffins. Across from where she was, there was a long bar that was surprisingly full of people. The restaurant was pretty packed.

I'm only going to sit here and wait for another ten minutes, then I'm leaving. This is ridiculous.

Calli sipped the water the waitress had left her before she turned her attention back to the menu in front of her. Derrick was right, the restaurant had an amazing menu. It was all organic and made from local and fresh ingredients. She could definitely get used to eating out at places like this.

Five minutes later, her father finally showed up.

"Sorry I'm so late, the photoshoot we were working on ran over." He cleared his throat and stood next to the table awkwardly for a moment before finally sitting down. Xander was attractive enough, although she was not sure what her mother had seen in him. He looked more like a school teacher or college professor than a photographer. His dark grey hair was well kept and he was clean-shaven. He wore a charcoal grey suit with a plain white shirt underneath. Compared to the other new people she had most recently met, he was downright boring and a little on the short side. He must have been just under six feet tall.

Calli smiled at him but did not say anything. The nerves that had been simmering just below the surface suddenly shot up to max level. She could tell that he was as nervous as she was now that he had arrived, but she was not going to make this any easier on him. He had had almost twenty-five years to find her, so a few more minutes of silence was not going to make any difference.

"So, how are you liking New York so far? Derrick said you seem to have adapted pretty quickly. He's quite impressed."

"Oh did he? Well, that's nice I suppose. New York is definitely interesting, but I am anxious to get everything wrapped up and return home." She sipped her water again, wondering where the waitress had disappeared to. Now that he had finally arrived she could hardly wait to be done and on her way.

"I understand how much of a shock this all is, and I can definitely see how getting everything wrapped up quickly will be a relief." He signaled for the waitress and ordered a scotch. As he settled back in his chair, she cleared her throat. "Oh, I'm sorry, did you want to order something?"

"No, I'm fine with water, but I know what I would like to order for dinner whenever you are ready." *You know, since I've been sitting here for at least twenty minutes.* She barely stifled the sigh that tried to slip out between her pressed lips.

"All right. I come here quite a bit so I know what I want as well. We can order when the waitress comes back with my drink."

Calli smiled tightly at him and nodded. "What are you going to order?" she asked.

"I was thinking we could order the bruschetta and the salmon car-paccio for our appetizers. Then for the first course, I personally like the pecorino and black pepper pasta. For the second course, I like the spigola, which is an amazing sea bass. The food here is on another level." He smiled.

"I'll probably have the fried market vegetables and then the peppered chicken. That sounds good. It smells amazing in here, so I'm excited to try the food."

"Okay, I will flag down the waitress." He raised his hand to get the waitress's attention and placed the order for them both while Calli sat back and observed him.

Her father was very polite to the waitress and immediately apologized to her for being late. She could tell he would be leaving the waitress a nice tip, and that helped thaw a bit of the ice surrounding her heart and her feelings about this whole matter.

After the waitress had written down their order and walked back to the kitchen, he turned back to her. "So, uh, tell me about you. How do you like living in Oregon? That is correct, right? You live with your Aunt Margaret?"

"Yes, I've lived with her since my mother passed away." *And you decided not to make it known that you are my father.* Calli cleared her throat and continued. "I graduated from Stanford with a Bachelor's degree in Environmental Science a few years ago, but I've been working with Aunt Maggie at her flower shop since then. I love it there. I can't wait to go back."

"That's good at least." He replied. "That you seem to be happy."

"Yes, I'm very happy with the life I have now."

Thankfully, after only a moment of awkward silence, the waitress dropped off their appetizers. She took a bite of the bruschetta and was instantly surprised by the taste of the tomatoes. It was as if she could taste the sunlight seeping into them as they grew on the vine. "Wow! This is amazingly good."

"It is, isn't it? This is by far my favorite restaurant in New York City."

"Did you travel a lot? Before coming back to New York, I mean?"

He smiled and nodded. "Yes, I've been able to travel all over the world. I used to do photojournalism, specifically covering wars. I've had work published with *National Geographic, Time,* and various newspapers. Now, I primarily do photoshoots with up and coming people for *GQ, Vogue,* etc."

She noticed a few of the waiters and waitresses gathering by the front door and the windows nearby. She couldn't see or hear what was causing them to gather there. "That, uh, sounds pretty...cool. It must have been fun to see the world, but sad as well given that you were covering wars. I've only seen California, Oregon, and New York myself. Although, New York has definitely changed since I was here last."

"Yeah, that happens in New York. It has a habit of changing when you leave and come back."

"Is that what happened? When my mother died? Were you away?"

The shocked look on his face was definitely worth asking those questions, even if it cost her a bit of her composure. Her voice nearly cracked when she said the last part. Tears welled in her eyes but, thankfully, stayed where they were.

"I, uh…Yes. I was in Iraq, I believe, when your mother passed away."

"Okay." She smiled sadly at him. "I mean, I don't forgive you for not being there for me. Like ever. I don't think I'll ever forgive you for what you've done. Or not done."

"I'm so sorry, Calliope. I didn't intend on waiting this long, but your mother…" He trailed off when the waitress came back to their table.

"I don't mean to interrupt you two, but we seem to have a bit of a situation going on out front. Apparently, the paparazzi have been notified you are here, and we suggest sneaking you out the back. Don't worry about paying for dinner. We've notified your driver, and he is waiting out back in the alley."

Calli looked at her father. "Does this happen often?"

"What? Me? No! I'm pretty sure they are here for you."

"Me? Why on earth would they want anything to do with me?"

The waitress interrupted. "You are Gabriella Morgan's daughter, aren't you? That's why they are all here. One of our other patrons must have recognized you and contacted the press. I'm so sorry about this, miss. I hope you will return again some time in the future."

"Oh, thank you. I'm sorry about this. I have no idea why they care if I'm here."

"It's fine! Just get out safely. Your mother was an inspiration to a lot of people. I think they are just excited to see you back home." She grabbed Calli's hand and squeezed it tightly, smiling warmly at her.

Her father stood up and ushered her to the back of the restaurant. They went through the kitchen, which was bustling with activity. It would have been highly interesting to stay and watch all the commotion, but she was at the back door faster than she could blink.

Xander grabbed her hand and pulled her in for a quick hug. "I'm so sorry about this. I will arrange dinner at my place or yours, whichever you prefer. I will get in contact with you as soon as possible. I'm so sorry." He kissed her gently on the forehead just as there was commotion at the entrance of the alleyway.

"There she is! Quick, everyone!" one of the paparazzi shouted.

Suddenly, there was a group of photographers rushing toward her as she stumbled into the car. Her father shut the door gently and knocked on the window to let the driver know he could take off. A second later, they sped through the alley, pushing through all the photographers trying to slow their progress.

Calli was definitely ready for an early bedtime after that disastrous dinner with her father. At least she had asked the question that had been bothering her since she had been requested to come to New York. Hopefully, she will get that answer sooner rather than later. If she had a child that was left alone after the child's father died, there was not anything on this earth that could keep her from them. Ideally, she would never be separated from them to begin with.

She tossed the key to the apartment onto the little oriental cabinet next to the door and wandered into the living room. Aretha had cleaned up the mess she had made of all of Calli's shoes, so they were all safe and secure in The Beast.

Calli stopped to set the Chanel purse on top of the coffee table before she wandered into the kitchen. Disappointment was definitely the theme for the night. She could not quite figure out if she was more displeased with her father, or disappointed that he had not given her a letter from her mother like the others had done.

Spinning the little carousel next to the coffee maker, she saw a container for some camomile tea and decided that was just what she needed. Grabbing a new mug from the cabinet nearest the coffee maker, she popped it under the little spigot. *I definitely need to get one of these for the flower shop. And my apartment. Aunt Maggie probably won't ever use it, but I love this thing.*

Leaning up against the kitchen counter, she sipped from the mug and started to make a mental note of what else needed to be accomplished on this trip. It seemed like she was almost done. She had met her father as her mother had asked, and she was sure she could have Aretha host an auction of some sort to sell the clothing and other items from her mother's closet. She would keep a few pieces, but definitely not all of them. There was not enough room in her closet back home, and she had no need for them.

The more she thought about it, the more she realized she needed to make a proper list of what needed to be done. She set her tea down on the counter and started opening up all the drawers in the kitchen. There just had to be a notepad and pen she could use to jot down the notes she had swirling in her head.

Not finding anything, she started to walk towards her luggage, but she took a few steps and the right heel of her shoe almost completely snapped off her Benedettos, causing her to lose her balance. As she tried to brace herself on the wall next to her, it completely gave way. She stumbled, breaking through the very thin wall and falling into the next apartment.

Chapter 7

Well, then. I guess I found that second apartment.

Coughing lightly from the dust and plaster from what appeared to be a thin fake wall behind her, she carefully stood up. The heel from her now-broken Benedettos dangled sadly as she pulled the pair of heels off.

"Damn it! It just had to be the Benedettos that broke didn't it!?" Calli grumbled angrily to herself as she took in her surroundings. She was in what appeared to be a workroom of some sort. Looking around, she found a light switch next to the opening she had fallen through and flipped the switch.

The hidden loft apartment had a completely open floor plan, except for the small bathroom and kitchen area on the opposite side from where she was standing. To her left were several racks of what appeared to be fabric and other sewing items like spools of thread and different types of needles. There were also several bookcases along the far wall full of books of all sizes, colors, and states of wear.

The rest of the apartment held various mannequins; each had a thin white silk sheet covering the clothing underneath. In the center of the room, there were several large tables that held two sewing machines, more fabric, and a stack of hardbound sketchbooks.

"This must be the studio she mentioned in her letter..." Calli said softly to herself. She started to walk towards the work tables in the center of the room so she could get a closer look at the sketchbooks when something caught her eye. Stopping, she turned slowly back to the bookcases behind her, shifting slightly as she saw something sparkle.

Setting the pair of Benedettos on the work table nearest to her, she wandered over to where she had seen the sparkle. There, on the top shelf of one of the bookcases, was a red box that had silver imprints on it. As she pulled the box from the shelf, she realized there was also a splash of silver iridescent stars across the box.

She walked back to the table where she had left the Benedettos and set this new box next to them. Carefully, she pulled the lid off and set it to the side. Inside she found a bunch of white tissue paper sprinkled with more opalescent stars. Pushing this carefully aside, she finally got to what was weighing the box down. Inside were two individually wrapped heels. She did not see a name on the lid or on the silver dust bags, so she grabbed one of the shoes and quickly unwrapped it.

They were absolutely amazing.

The red patent leather of the heels was by far the best she had ever seen or felt. She could tell that whoever made them had spent a lot of time carefully creating them. As she tilted the shoe to inspect the bottom, she was surprised to see stainless steel stars of various sizes sprinkled all along the underside of the heel. They sparkled against the dark black of the under-sole when they caught the light from overhead.

These were the most beautiful shoes she had ever seen.

Eagerly, she angled the shoes so that she was able to inspect the inside and gasped with excitement. They're Benedettos. Oh my god, these are unbelievable.

She saw that they were her size and, without any hesitation, she slid the first heel onto her bare foot. It fit perfectly. Like the shoe designer himself had made a mold of her exact foot and made this shoe just for her.

Laughter bubbled up as she hurried to pull the other shoe from the silver dust bag. Impatiently, she got the shoe onto her foot. It felt the same as the other—like she was destined to have these shoes. She stood absolutely still for a moment, memorizing how perfect these shoes felt on her feet.

"Calli?! Where on earth are you, child! I heard the most horrendous crash! And some other horrible noise! Did you scream or something?" Aretha called from her front door.

Calli could hear her FGM coming toward her, but she did not move. She was too busy savoring the feel of the shoes on her feet.

"What on earth is going on!?" Aretha asked as she stepped into the second apartment, careful to avoid the large pieces of the thin wall that were still hanging haphazardly in the opening.

Tonight her FGM was all about a '50s theme. Her hair was in a traditional bouffant style and she had a sleeveless '50s-style dress that had a huge poofy skirt that rested just above her knees. She was wearing a pair of Charlotte Olympia Party Girl pumps. And of course, the dress and shoes were pink—as usual. Her makeup was styled with the classic cat-eye and red lip common in that era.

The minute she saw what Calli was wearing on her feet, Aretha stopped and took a steadying breath. "Where on earth did you find those?" Her eyes were wide with shock.

"Oh, they were in a box on that shelf over there." She half-heartedly pointed to where she had found them. "Aren't they beautiful?! They've even got stars on the bottom! And they are Benedettos! Oh my gosh, I've always wanted a pair of red ones!"

Aretha paled when she heard 'stars'. "Calli, listen to me, darling. You have to take those shoes off. Right now!"

Calli frowned at her. "Oh, but why? They're gorgeous and they fit me perfectly! And I just broke my only pair of Benedettos... It's like I was meant to find these amazing shoes!" She still did not move as she seemed frozen to the spot.

Aretha came over to where she stood and carefully grasped her by the shoulders. "Calli, please take them off, and I will explain everything to you. Those shoes are cursed!"

Calli gasped. "Wait—cursed? What do you mean?"

"Please just take them off and I'll explain everything. I promise."

She could tell that Aretha was seriously frightened. Not fully understanding what the problem was, Calli nodded. "Oh, okay. One second."

Calli slowly pulled the exquisite shoes off, placed them in their dust bags, and carefully stored them in their box just as she had found them. She immediately felt the sadness of the horrible dinner with her father and the overwhelming situation she was in crash right back into her. Taking a slow and shaky breath, she stared at Aretha.

"Explain."

"Oh, child. Don't you know your fairy tales? Those are *The Shoes*!"

"The what? I mean, of course they're shoes." Calli looked at her quizzically.

"No! Not shoes, THE SHOES! Please tell me you've heard of them." Aretha stomped her feet in frustration.

"No. I have no idea what you are talking about."

"Oh my goodness! What am I going to do with you?!" She frowned at Calli. "Here, go sit in your mother's apartment on the couch while I go get some things, and then I'll explain everything."

"Sure, okay." Calli took the red box and carefully placed her broken pair of Benedettos on top of it. Following Aretha out through the gaping hole and back into her mother's apartment, she set the box and broken shoes on the coffee table. She grabbed the still-warm cup of tea and curled up on the couch.

After a few minutes, Aretha returned with three white boxes of varying sizes in her arms. She handed them to Calli as she sat down next to her on the couch. "There! Now you will have a phone and a laptop so you will be able to get ahold of me or anyone else you may need to get into contact with."

She pointed to the larger of the three boxes. "Hand me the laptop, sweetie, and we will get started on your education about *The Shoes*." When she said *The Shoes*, she spoke in a deep, spooky voice.

Calli obliged and handed her the larger of the boxes.

It was one of the latest Apple macbooks. She smiled sheepishly at Calli. "I hope you don't mind me setting this up for you, but we need to get on YouTube so I can show you a couple videos."

"Oh no, I don't mind at all." She sat back and waited patiently for Aretha to get everything set up and ready to go. "In fact, thank you so much for purchasing these for me. You really didn't need to."

"Oh, child, don't worry about it! You can consider these the presents for all the birthdays and Christmases I've missed." She reached over and patted Calli's knee. "You don't have WiFi in this apartment, but I'm able to connect to mine. We will get the WiFi set up for you here in the next few days."

Calli nodded and picked up the medium-sized box and opened it. Inside was one of the newest Apple iPhones. She turned it on, but knew she would definitely need Aretha's help getting it configured, so she set it and the box on the table. She had not owned a cell phone since she graduated college. She was always with her aunt or made sure to tell her exactly where she was going.

The smallest of the boxes held a red leather case for her new phone. She slid the leather case onto the new phone, and then set it back on the coffee table.

"Alrighty then, here we go!" Aretha placed the laptop on the coffee table and opened up YouTube.

"Ooh, this is a good one! So absolutely tragic." Selecting the video entitled 'The Shoes - Designer Has Disastrous Fashion Show!', she set it to fullscreen before sitting back to watch.

The video showed a young male designer walking down the runway with a model at the end of his show. The model was wearing The Shoes and seemed to be more than a little nervous. When they had reached the top of the runway, the designer gestured to the model to walk down the runway again, and she obliged begrudgingly. But, as she was walking back up the second time, she slipped and fell backward. One of the shoes shot off her foot, hitting the designer right in the middle of his forehead.

"That designer, to this day, still has an imprint of the stars from the bottom of *The Shoes* on his forehead. And the model has retired from the runway and works at her family's restaurant now. I don't necessarily blame her." Aretha shook her head.

"We tried to warn the designer that he shouldn't use *The Shoes* in his show, but he was stubborn and wouldn't listen to us. I bet he regrets it now. I think he works as a tailor back home in Illinois."

"Hmm, okay... What does that have to do with The Shoes though? This doesn't really explain anything."

"Sorry, darling, I thought there would be a video explaining the history of *The Shoes*. Maybe I'll do one!" She laughed to herself. "That's why, if you search 'The Shoes' on YouTube, all these famous disasters will come up. I mean, look at them all!" She scrolled through all the different videos. There were at least fifty, if not more.

"So, what's the deal with these shoes?"

"I know you are familiar with the shoe designer Arturo Benedetto. He retired about fifteen years ago or so, but before he officially retired, he made *The Shoes*. They were meant to be his finalé. His final masterpiece. Arturo has since disappeared, so it's not like we can ask him what happened or why."

Aretha reached and picked up the broken pair of Benedettos, placing them carefully on the coffee table. "I know a wonderful shoe cobbler that will be able to repair those for you." She smiled brightly at Calli. "No worries, dear."

She then opened the box and pulled one of the wrapped heels out, carefully unwrapping it. "It really is a shame no one can wear these gorgeous shoes." She turned to Calli and smiled sadly. "You see, they're cursed."

"Yeah, you mentioned that. But you didn't explain why or anything."

"Arturo created these shoes to be worn by the person that would be responsible for issuing a new renaissance of fashion and beauty into the industry. We all love the current designers and retailers, but it's a bit... stagnant. *The Shoes* are supposed to foretell that there will be a breath of fresh air in the industry, but unfortunately, a lot of designers decided to take *The Shoes* and force it." Aretha carefully inspected the shoe in her hand before turning back to Calli.

"No one knows for sure how they came to be cursed exactly. Some think it was because of all the designers and models who tried to become 'The Chosen' ones. That they are responsible for all the bad things that have happened to those who tried to force it. I, however, think they possess a bit of magic, and are meant to be for only one person."

"So, basically, if anyone wears them or incorporates them in any way into their show or whatever, they'll have a bad go of it?"

"Essentially. This is why you have to be super careful with them. I wouldn't wear them out of this apartment, that's for sure. I wouldn't wear them at all if I were you." She nodded sagely as she set the beautiful shoe on the table. "If anyone were to find out you have them, they would be hounding you to try and see them—or possibly even steal them. There's a huge collection of people on the internet that to this day are trying to track them down. I wonder if your mother left them here."

"I would like to say no, she wouldn't do that, but honestly—who knows?" Calli frowned. "I didn't even know about this second apartment. My mother never said anything to me about it. And I definitely don't remember her going into this other apartment. But I wasn't always with her. Or possibly she would go work in there after I was asleep. It seems like she might have been working on something. Maybe a collection of sorts or something?"

"Really? Interesting! She never mentioned anything to me either. Want to go have a look and see what she made?" Aretha clapped her hands with giddiness.

"Sure. Why not?" Calli smiled as she got up off the couch. "I'm going to need to get some slippers or something. I can't keep wearing my heels everywhere."

"We can go get some tomorrow! Gary and I can also finally take you to Sephora." Aretha did a little shimmy when she said Sephora, like she was like going to a huge party or something. Calli giggled, her excitement was infectious. "And since Sephora is right by Macy's, we can stop by there!"

They carefully stepped over the plaster and into the newly found apartment. "I'll call maintenance tomorrow to come over and take care of this hole. There's no reason for it to be there any longer I don't think!"

Calli nodded and made her way over to the mannequins. There were eleven total that were all dressed in different outfits underneath the thin silk sheet that protected them from the dust in the apartment. Although, there wasn't much dust at all. It was like the apartment had been sealed to prevent anything from possibly damaging the items.

There was also a group of mannequins that were basically naked, gathered in the far corner next to the huge floor-to-ceiling windows. She couldn't wait to see what the apartment would look like once the sunlight was streaming in through those windows.

Walking up to the nearest mannequin, she carefully removed the silk cloth covering the garment hidden beneath the creamy white fiber. The mannequin was adorned in an unbelievably beautiful dress that somehow reminded Calli of sweet peas. The top was a soft pink corset and the full knee-length skirt bloomed out from the waist. The interesting thing about the dress is that the full skirt was made up of five folded 'petals', just like a sweet pea.

Aretha appeared next to Calli and spun the mannequin slowly so that the skirt flared out beautifully. "This is absolutely stunning. My goodness! I had no idea your mother was interested in or capable of creating something so gorgeous!"

"I know what you mean! Although honestly, she was always sketching and drawing, so this doesn't surprise me in the least."

Aretha took a few steps to the next mannequin and carefully removed the silk covering. This dress was completely white and had five different triangle-like sections that made up the top. There was one for the front, one for each arm, and two that made up the back. The simple short pencil skirt was impeccably made, regardless of the simplicity of it. Instantly, Calli thought of the flower stephanotis.

Calli walked to the next mannequin and pulled the cover from it eagerly. Underneath was a deep red and green skirt and top set that reminded her of a red tulip. The top had a tight waist that bloomed into the typical fullness of the tulip around the bust, leaving the shoulders bare. Another pencil skirt in a deep green, but this one fell completely to the floor.

"These are amazing. Seriously." Aretha went to the next covered outfit. You could barely see bright pink shining through the soft silk hiding it. When her FGM pulled the silk away, the room burst into light from the dress beneath. It was a hot pink dress that had groups of the silk in bunches throughout the full dress. The bunches started out larger and fuller on the bottom, and thinned out toward the top. "What does this remind you of?" Aretha paused, looking at the dress carefully as she spun it.

"Hmm... Maybe the flower gladiolus? See how it has all these different bunches? Gladioli have a bunch of different flowers on each stem. It's kind of like an explosion of flowers. Does that make sense?"

"Definitely! I'm not super familiar with flowers, but we can look them up on the internet once we have them all uncovered."

The next mannequin had what appeared to be a deep purple color under the silk covering it. Calli pulled the silk sheet away and gasped. This dress was definitely inspired by hibiscus flowers, but not just the single-colored ones, the multicolored ones. It had a deep purple corset top, and then the same purple bled into a bright purple at the bottom of the full skirt.

"She'd better have more pink here!" Aretha exclaimed as she pulled off the next cover and gasped happily.

More hot pink flooded into their vision. "This one is definitely plumeria!" Calli clapped happily. The bright pink fitted top bled into five triangles that made up the skirt. Aretha squealed as she spun this new dress, and, as the skirt flared out, you could see hints of bright yellow.

"This one has to be fuchsia, for sure! And it's pink again, Aretha." Calli called as she uncovered the next dress. It was a deep pink that started out as a corseted top and the skirt had multiple short layers in varying shades of the same pink, identical to the fuchsia flower.

The next piece was similar to the fuchsia dress, but instead of the alternating shades of pink, the corseted bodice was a bright golden yellow. The skirt was white but each 'petal' that made up the skirt was a long strip that ended with a slight dip. "This one is inspired by a daisy, absolutely!" Calli spun this one to see how the petals flared out, making the dress look exactly like a daisy.

Aretha uncovered another pink and white dress. The top was a bright pink that faded into the white skirt, which ended just below the knees. It was undoubtedly a geranium.

The last two pieces were, sadly, unfinished. They were obviously meant to be rose-themed dresses. Calli could see the shape in the white and red fabric that was strung on the completed tops of each dress. However, the individual 'petals' that made up the skirt were just pinned on.

"Oh, these aren't finished! That's such a shame." Calli said as she ran her fingers down the fabric of the red one. "I bet I could finish them..."

"Really? I think you should!"

Calli looked over at Aretha. "What are you thinking about?"

Aretha was standing next to the two rose-themed dresses, one hand on her hip and the other resting on her chin. She tapped her perfectly manicured pointer finger on her lip a moment before moving to spin the white rose dress very slowly on the mannequin.

She looked up at Calli, her eyes bright with happiness. "We should host a show. These are too beautiful to keep a secret. We could do it in honor of your mother."

"Um, okay. I have no idea how to do that though."

"Oh don't worry, darling! I can help for sure! I have all kinds of contacts in the fashion industry. I am a Fairy God Mother after all!"

Calli looked at how excited her FGM was and didn't have the heart to say no. "Okay... Well, what do we need to do to do all that?"

Aretha came over and put her hand on her shoulder. "I know you've had a really hard day today, so don't worry about it tonight. We will get started over the next few days. I am going to need to get a new planner tomorrow so I can get everything all planned out. Your mother's designs will be in very good hands!"

Chapter 8

"Rise and shine, dear! We can't keep Fairy Gary and Sephora waiting." Aretha burst into her bedroom and pushed back the curtains covering the window so the early morning light streamed into the room.

Calli still could not sleep in her mother's bed, so she had been sleeping in her old bedroom. Aretha came over and tore the covers off of Calli, then put her hands on her hips. "Come on. Get up! I hope you don't mind, but I decided to come over and raid your mother's closet. For you, of course!"

Calli chuckled and slipped out of bed. As she followed Aretha into her mother's closet, she pulled at her I Love New York t-shirt. "Maybe I can get some legit pajamas, too, while we are out today?"

"Of course! We can do whatever you wish!" Aretha started to go through the rack of dresses nearest the door so Calli took a moment to take in her outfit. Today she was sporting a very clever and sharp suit. Instead of a button-up top, she had on a loose white camisole. And, of course, the suit was in the same shade of pale pink that her FGM was prone to wear. Her long blond hair was pulled back into a high ponytail that was bound up with a thick piece of silk that matched the suit perfectly. Her shoes were a classy pair of black Louboutin Jonatina leather sandals.

"I'm gonna go brush my teeth and stuff while you check the closet. I assume you'll pick out something gorgeous for me to wear." She chuckled softly.

"Obviously, dear! Every article of clothing here in this closet is beautiful. It would be a very sad day indeed if there was something plain or boring in here."

"So, what's the plan today?" Calli called from the bathroom as she brushed her teeth.

"We are going to go to Sephora and Macy's! They are pretty close together. And then we can go by Bryant Park! We won't be able to get in to see any of the shows going on during Fashion Week, but I still think you'd like to see it."

"Oh, yes! That would be very cool I think," Calli said as she walked back into the closet.

Aretha had a selection of her mother's Diane Von Furstenberg vintage print dresses draped casually over her arm. She gestured to them as she said, "I figured today we would inject a bit of color into your life! What better way than with some DVF wrap dresses? These are absolutely to die for!"

Aretha took the four dresses she had and handed the hangers to Calli. "Go! Try these on."

Calli took the dresses and went back into the bathroom. The first was a lovely royal blue and white sleeveless wrap dress with ginkgo leaves scattered all over it. Next, she had selected a bright green short-sleeved dress that had white stalks of bamboo. There was also a brilliant purple dress with white geometric patterns on it. And last but certainly not least was a red sleeveless dress with a funky flower-inspired pattern in white.

She took off the T-shirt she was wearing and slipped into the green wrap dress right away. She loved the way the bamboo stalks were situated on the piece. Of all the colors Aretha had chosen, she was partially drawn to the green because it would look best with her pale complexion, green eyes, and red hair.

Stepping back into the closet, she did a little spin and curtsy. "I think this is the one!"

Aretha clapped in agreement. "Now, darling, let us go find you some shoes in that magical trunk of yours. I think those black Louboutin Pigalles will be just the thing! Especially since your Benedettos are broken. Remind me when we get back to have them sent out to be repaired."

As they walked back into the living room, there was a soft knock on the door. "Ooh! Fairy Gary is here!" Aretha shooed Calli to go answer the door.

"Hello, Gary. Thank you for coming over to join us shopping. I think we will have fun!" Calli smiled brightly at him.

Hee was dressed as impeccably today as the first day she met him. She was starting to realize this is always how he dressed. He was wearing a sharp silver three piece suit, which was tailored to perfection—just like the last suit she had seen him in. His tie and handkerchief were the exact same shade of pink as the suit Aretha was wearing. He looked absolutely dashing.

"Hello, Calli. I'm sure we will most certainly have fun. We are going shopping after all, and how could shopping not be considered fun?" He smiled wryly.

They walked into the living room together, but as soon as Gary saw The Shoes on the coffee table, he stopped. His smile disappeared, and he turned almost as white as the shirt he was wearing. "Where..." He cleared his throat and tried again. "Where on earth did *those* come from? Those are *The Shoes*, aren't they?" He took a purposeful step back away from them.

"Oh! I found those in the apartment next door." Calli gestured to the misshapen hole in the wall. "That reminds me! I need to call Kenneth and let him know I've located it." She took the shoe from the coffee table and returned it to its dust bag and placed it carefully back in the box.

"You should go look in there, Gary. There's a bunch of different dresses my mother apparently made. Aretha suggested that we should host a fashion show or something."

Gary was frozen to his spot. He looked incredulously between Calli and Aretha, who was currently going through The Beast to find the Pigalles she mentioned earlier.

Aretha gave a shout of success and stood up with the shoes hooked by the heel in each hand. She walked over to where Gary and Calli were standing. "What's with him?" she asked, handing her the Pigalles.

Calli sat on the couch to put them on and shrugged. "I have no idea! It probably has something to do with The Shoes." She got the last heel on and looked up between the two of them. "I think he's broken."

Gary visibly shook himself and sat down on the edge of the couch. "Aretha. Please tell me those aren't what I think they are."

"Oh, they are. Undeniably so. Did you want to see them? They really are on a whole other level of gorgeousness."

"Um, no. I like my life just the way it is. I will not be touching those. Ever."

Calli chuckled. "I mean, they are just shoes, Gary. I wore them last night for a bit, and I'm still here and completely okay."

Gary shook his head incredulously at her. "You are definitely braver than I am. I honestly don't even like being in the same room as them! No! The same building. Those shoes are cursed!" He gave himself another little shake and composed himself before standing up. "Alright, you two crazy kids. Let's get going. Sephora is calling! And the further I can get away from *those*, the better." He shot The Shoes an incredulous look before walking out the front door.

Their shopping trip was a huge success, and the bags they were all carrying as they walked back to Aretha's car were the evidence. They first went to Macy's and found a set of adorable sushi pajamas and a pair of black and white slippers. Each slipper looked like a fuzzy panda, and they even had a little poof for the tail.

Next, they spent a good part of the morning at Sephora, where Gary filled her in on all the things in makeup, hair care, and skincare that Calli had no idea she was missing. She had picked up a couple of the different eyeshadow pallets that were insanely popular from Too Faced and Urban Decay. The store had sold out of one of the pallets Calli wanted, but Gary promised he had a new one in his studio she could have. Gary may give off the impression that he was a block of ice with little to no emotion, but underneath she could see that he was actually very warm and giving. You just had to get under that cold prickly exterior first.

After they had loaded all their shopping bags into the trunk of Aretha's car, they climbed in. Gary let her sit in the passenger seat and handed her a hair tie that she could have sworn appeared out of thin air. "Here. You're going to need this. Aretha is planning on putting the top down."

Calli thanked him and put her hair up into a high ponytail like Aretha's. "Oh, Aretha, I meant to ask, does your car have a name?" She asked as she secured her seatbelt.

"Of course she does!" Aretha patted the steering wheel apologetically. "Calli, this is Betty. Betty, this is Calli! She's the daughter of Miss Gabriella. You remember her, I'm sure."

Gary strapped himself in and pulled out a pair of classic Louis Vuitton sunglasses and put them on.

"All right, Betty! Let's get this top off!" Aretha turned to Calli and asked, "Could you pull that lever on your side? See, it looks like this one." She showed Calli what she was talking about on her side and pulled the little lever.

Calli found the lever on her side of the car and pulled it like Aretha showed her.

Aretha pushed one of the many dials on the dash and the top started to go down. It reminded Calli of a butterfly opening its wings. "Everyone strapped in?" They both nodded, so Aretha pulled out of the parking spot.

"We are just going to drive by where Fashion Week is," Aretha said loudly over the rumble of the Cadillac and the noise of the city.

"Okay, that sounds good to me! Thank you for taking me by, Aretha."

As they got nearer to Bryant Park, the crowds of people grew exponentially. When they finally drove by the center of all the activity, she could see white pop-up tents scattered around the outside of the building. Aretha spoke as she maneuvered the car down the street. "This used to be where all the different fashion houses would host their shows. In the last few years, they have all branched out and will basically host their show wherever they can find a place willing. There have even been a few shows in Central Park."

"That's pretty cool! I kinda wish we could go see a show. Aren't you my Fairy God Mother? Can't you get tickets or something?" Calli asked teasingly.

"Oh, child, I would move heaven and earth to be able to get you in. It's just simply not possible! I can definitely get you in to see a few shows next year though—that is if you will be back in New York then. Even Fairy God Mothers need a bit more than a few days' notice."

Calli laughed, "It's okay, Aretha. I'll forgive you, especially if we can go shopping again before I leave. I think you are my good luck charm."

"Of course I am, dear! I can't be a Fairy God Mother without having a bit of luck to share. Now, let's get back to the apartment before poor Fairy Gary melts. It is a tad warm out here today." Aretha chuckled to herself. Gary was in the backseat fanning himself with a cute fan that matched his silver suit. Calli was beginning to believe he had secret pockets.

As the three of them walked down the hallway, they saw someone sitting on the floor next to Calli's apartment door. When she got closer, she recognized him.

"Hey, Derrick, what's up? I hope you haven't been waiting long."

"Oh no, I got here just a few minutes ago. I literally just sat down, so no worries." He said as he got up off the floor.

"See! Now I know what all the fuss is about!" Aretha exclaimed as she looked him up and down.

Calli rolled her eyes and laughed. "Just ignore her, okay?" She said to Derrick as she unlocked the apartment door. "Come on in. We were going to go through all the stuff in the next apartment. Apparently, my mother was creating a clothing collection before she passed away and told no one about it—even me. I found it last night."

"Ah, okay. I came by to see if you wanted to go see one of Roland Arsenault's photography exhibits with me. But we can go another time." He looked more than a little disappointed.

"Goodness me, no! You two go on. It's no big deal!" Aretha exclaimed.

They all entered the apartment together. Calli couldn't help but notice that Gary went to sit on the farthest part of the couch away from The Shoes. She shook her head but did not say anything.

"Let me just grab a purse, do something with my hair, switch shoes, and then we can go, okay?" Calli said as she went over to The Beast. She loved the Pigalles, but they were not very comfortable to wear for long periods of time and she had already been shopping in them. The last thing her feet would appreciate is walking around an art gallery in them too.

Aretha looked over to where Derrick was standing in the doorway with a mischievous grin on her face. "What is it you do, Derrick? I think Calli mentioned you were her father's assistant or something?"

"Uh, yeah, that's exactly what I do. It's been pretty great to be honest. Calli's father is an amazing photographer. I've learned a ton." He shot Calli a 'help me!' look. She just smiled and mouthed, 'Sorry, one second!'

She ran into the bathroom to quickly take her hair out of the high ponytail she had put it in. She was shocked that her hair looked pretty good. There were a few curls to rearrange, but it would definitely pass.

Running back into the living room, Calli grabbed the Ferragamo Vara pumps she had worn the day she met with Kenneth. They were honestly the most comfortable pair of shoes she had with her now.

"Alright, let's go," she said as she picked up the Chanel purse that she had used last night. Her wallet was still in it.

"Oh! Here's your new phone, Calli. Please don't forget it." Aretha said as she handed it to her.

"Thanks, Aretha." She smiled as she took the phone.

"All right, children, have a ton of fun! We'll have our own little adventure next door looking through all the goodies your mom has stashed there." She winked.

Calli laughed as she and Derrick walked out the door.

Chapter 9

"How long have you been working for my father? I don't think I've asked you that yet." She laughed awkwardly as they walked up to the gallery.

"I've been his assistant since I graduated from college, so…about three years?" He looked confused for a second, then nodded. "Yeah. Three years. Wow, I can't believe it's been that long." He chuckled softly to himself.

"Time flies when you're having fun, right?"

"Yeah, I suppose it does." He smiled at her before turning to the gallery door and opening it for her. "Here we are."

"Thank you." She smiled at him briefly before walking in. The gallery was a very large space, and each wall held a variety of different sized images. Some were small eight-by-ten-inch prints, and some were bigger, twenty-by-thirty sized. There was even a large installation of images that stretched from the floor to the ceiling and across the entire space where the exhibit was being held.

Calli went up to the first large photograph. It was of a female model in an amazing black and white long dress posing in a luxurious position. But she was standing in front of several elephants. The contrast between the beauty of the model and her dress next to the roughness of the elephants was a wonderful juxtaposition.

Wandering from one photograph to the next, she was astounded. Every image was in black and white, but they spoke to her in so much color. As she looked at each print, she could imagine all the hard work and effort it took just to capture each photograph.

"You like them then?" asked Derrick quietly from behind her. He had let her wander about taking in the different images.

"Oh, yes! These are amazing!" She pointed to the one of the model Twiggy in the midst of a whirlwind of her own hair as though she had been bending down then flung her head back dramatically. "I've seen this one before! I've actually seen a lot of these before. I just had no idea they were all taken by the same man."

"Yes, he was quite popular." He smiled and took her hand. "Here, there's one I've been wanting to show you."

They rounded the corner of the very back of the exhibit. There hung another one of the larger than life images. It took up the whole section of the back wall. The image showed a model mid-spin in front of the Washington Square Park arch. Calli could feel the joy and exhilaration of the model and could almost picture her happily spinning in her head.

Stepping closer to the photograph, Calli realized she recognized the model.

"Is that…" Clearing her throat, she attempted to speak again. "Is that my…" She gasped softly before the words finally tumbled out. "Is that my mother?"

"It is. I thought you should see it. There's a few of her here actually. I'll point them out if you'd like. This is one of his most popular pieces."

"I uh…I mean, no it's um…it's okay." She slowly let her fingers slip from his hand and she turned to smile briefly at him. "I actually, um, I have to go." She blinked quickly to keep the tears from falling.

"Oh man. I'm so sorry, Calli. I should have warned you about her images here. I am so, so sorry. I thought you would be excited to see them. Want to go get a coffee or something?" He smiled sheepishly and offered his hand to her.

She shook her head and started to head toward what she believed was the exit, almost running directly into another photograph of her mother. This next image was of her jumping from the curb into a busy New York side street with an umbrella in her hand. She gasped and turned away, but was face-to-face with yet another image of her mother.

This photograph was captured in still life. It featured Gabriella in head-to-toe Dior, and she was apparently chasing after a cab, capturing her mid-run on the streets of New York. She looked as though she was flying.

Each of the photographer's images had her mother in motion. It was quintessentially her—Calli remembered she was almost never still when she had been alive. Even in her sleep, she still moved. Calli would sneak into her bedroom to cuddle with her and she kept tossing and turning until Calli woke her up. Oddly enough, as she was circled in her arms, her mother stayed still.

Calli gasped again, taking all the other images in for a moment before turning into Derrick. "I really do have to go. I'm so sorry. I'll, uh…I'll talk to you tomorrow." She ducked under his arms as he tried to hold onto her and darted toward the entrance. The tear drops falling on the ground as she fled from the gallery left a sad little trail on the sidewalk.

Calli ran from the gallery on foot. She did not even glance at the driver her father had hired for her, so intent was her desperation to flee from the gallery. He was taking a break, standing next to the car on his phone the moment she burst out of the gallery. He called after her in confusion, but she continued her escape.

She only stopped running because she could not breathe anymore. Stumbling to her knees, she caught herself on a wrought iron gate. After a few moments of gulping in as much air as she possibly could, she looked up to take in her surroundings.

She was on the sidewalk in between two tall multistory buildings. The wrought iron gate she caught herself on appeared to open up to a garden in the alleyway. All the green surprised Calli—it was full of different plants. The only 'blank' space in the garden was the brick pathway. She supposed it had been a plain boring alleyway at one point, but she imagined the people in the area coming together to build a little green oasis inside the bustling city. It was wonderful and almost reminded her of the alleyway gardens in Oregon.

Inside the garden, there were several wrought iron benches. Calli got up, dusted off her knees, and headed over to the nearest bench. She sat down heavily, resting her head in her hands.

This whole situation in New York was becoming way too much. Meeting her father had been an absolute nightmare, and she still had not heard from him at all. He could have called to make sure she got back to the apartment okay—or something. Fathers usually like to check up on their daughters. At least according to all the sappy father and daughter movies she had seen over her twenty-five years.

Calli reached up to wipe the tears away that had been streaming down her face. She knew that he did not realize seeing her mother's photographs would upset her so much. Hopefully he would forgive her for abandoning him like that.

Really the only highlight of this entire trip had been her FGMs. Her Fairy *Freaking* God Mothers. How absolutely random was that? Aretha was just plain amazing, and Gary was probably the most loyal person she had ever met. She truly felt blessed having both of them in her life now. She would be sad to leave them when she went home.

Just then, she realized she had not called her Aunt Maggie at all since she had arrived in New York. "Oh crap!" she said to herself as she grabbed her purse to find the phone that Aretha had given her. It was still early evening, and with the time difference, it would be the perfect time to speak to her aunt. She dialed Maggie's number and was surprised when her aunt's name popped up. Aretha must have pre-programmed the numbers for her.

"Um, hello? I don't recognize this number so I don't know who this is. Hopefully you aren't one of those telemarketer type people 'cause I don't have a credit card or anything, and I'm not giving you my checking account information. Or my social security number. You'll get nothing! Absolutely nothing from me!"

"Aunt Maggie? Hi! It's Calli! How are you? How are things going at the flower shop? Everything going okay?" Calli laughed quietly to herself and leaned back against the bench she was sitting on.

"Calli! Hello, my darling girl! How is New York treating you? Have you met your father yet?"

"Um…it's been weird to be honest. I did meet my father—oh jeez, was that only yesterday? So much has happened but it seems like time is standing still…. Does that even make sense?" she asked halfheartedly.

"Of course it does, of course. I can only imagine what you are going through there." She paused for a moment before asking, "Do you think you'll be coming home soon?"

"Well, here's the thing, Aunt Maggie. Apparently, Mom was secretly designing her own line of clothes, and I found it all yesterday after dinner with my father. I think Aretha mentioned she wants to do a fashion show or something with the designs I found so I think I have to stay to see that all finished. But then I'm definitely coming home. How are things going in the shop? Everything okay?"

"Oh! Everything's wonderful! Mr. Bronson came in to get a congratulations bouquet for his wife! They are expecting a little one soon! All those 'I'm Sorry' bouquets must have worked their magic!"

"Oh, that's great! Please tell him congratulations!"

"I definitely will, dear. Did you know Mrs. Leland's son is back from college? He graduated summa cum laude from Stanford. He said he was looking for a job and heard you were away for a bit, so I think I'm going to hire him until you get back."

"Oh, really?" Calli giggled. "It doesn't have anything to do with how attractive he is?"

"Oh pish posh! He's got a girlfriend! And besides, I'm old enough to be his grandmother..." she added under her breath, "It's not my fault he fills out those jeans so perfectly."

"My gosh, Aunt Maggie! You need a boyfriend!"

"Definitely not! I'm too set in my ways. I'll just stare happily at the tasty treats here in our little town." She giggled wickedly. "Speaking of nice butts, how is that boy that came to take you to New York? What was his name again?"

"Derrick. His name is Derrick." Calli tried to keep the sadness out of her voice. She did not want to tell her aunt about what happened tonight. Aunt Maggie would most likely be upset that she had gotten so overwhelmed and ran away.

"Ah yes, Derrick! He was a tasty treat! Get in that!"

Calli busted out laughing again.

"Wait! Did I say it wrong? What is it you young kids say?"

"I think it's 'get *on* that', but I have no idea. It's not something I'd ever say." Calli laughed again. This was just what she needed.

"I'm so sorry I haven't called, Aunt Maggie. Things have been a whirlwind here for me. I think things will settle down soon though. I'll call you in a couple days to let you know when I think I'll be coming home, okay?"

"No problem, darling. Everything is going smoothly here, so no worries. I miss you, though! I'm going to have to hire some kids to clean up the shop before you get home, so just make sure to give me a couple days' notice."

Calli ran her hand across her face and replied, "Seriously?"

"No, of course not! Just my areas in the shop are their typical mess. I know how much order and cleanliness makes you happy, dear."

"Thank you, Aunt Maggie. You are seriously the best."

"I know, dear! I'm gonna go now; there's a new show on TV that is premiering tonight and it looks super interesting!"

"Okay, Aunt Maggie. You'll have to tell me all about it when I get back home."

"Certainly! Have a good night, Calli!"

"Goodnight, Aunt Maggie."

She ended the call and slipped the phone back into her purse. Taking a deep breath, she leaned against the bench and rested her arms on the back. She needed to figure out where the hell she was so she could find her way back to her mother's apartment. Taking another deep breath, she got back onto her feet and headed back toward the street.

It looked like she was in a very nice neighborhood. The huge buildings that surrounded her just seemed to scream 'money'. Every building was brick, and even though there was not a lot of space for greenery, every section of empty space had some kind of plant or landscaping done.

As she took in her surroundings, a flash of red caught her eye. It was not the red of the flashing neon 'OPEN' sign, but the bright, vibrant red of fabric dancing in the wind directly across the street. It seemed to call to her.

The red fabric was on one of the large spools sitting in a wire mesh fabric bin along with several other types of fabric. As she got closer, she realized it was sitting outside a fabric store named Giuseppe's Fabrics.

Almost in a daze, she walked closer to the bin. Her hand was shaking as she reached out to touch the fabric. She unwrapped a bit of it so she could run it across her cheek. The light cloth was slightly stiff but also smooth. It was a beautiful red silk organza. She absolutely had to have it.

Grabbing the spool, she placed it haphazardly over her shoulder to bring it inside. Happily, the door swung into the little shop.

"Hello? Is there anyone here? I would very much like to purchase this fabric." She stood at the entrance while she took in her surroundings. It was a small store and it was absolutely packed with every kind of fabric and sewing accessory imaginable—from heavy suedes to the lightest of silks in a variety of colors. It would take her several hours to make it through the little shop and see everything.

To her left was a little counter that held a very ornate antique cash register. It was silver in color and had beautiful filigree scrollwork all across it. It even had a placard across the top that read 'Amount Purchased', and had a little window where the total would pop up. She hoped it still worked.

She shifted the spool of fabric to her other shoulder.

"Hello?" she called out.

Suddenly an older gentleman appeared next to her. "Gabriella, dear! Is that you?"

Chapter 10

He grabbed the pair of glasses on a thin silver chain around his neck and quickly put them on. "Oh dear! I'm so very sorry! You actually aren't who I thought you were at all."

"Did you say Gabriella?" She cleared her throat. "Did you mean Gabriella Morgan by any chance?

"Why yes! I'm sorry I mistook you for her! She passed away some years ago sadly. It's funny how you see someone or something and all the memories come rushing back!" He smiled brightly at her a moment before shuffling over to the embellished cash register. "Now, what can I do for you, young lady?"

As he walked by her, she realized he was a very slight gentleman. She was probably only an inch or so taller than him. She saw that he had what she assumed was a pocket watch on a chain that went from one of the button holes on his tweed vest to one of the pockets. His shoes were worn, but you could tell he took great care of them, probably shining them every night before wearing them the next day. His hair was light gray, and although similar to Gary's in color, it was very fuzzy and stuck up in all directions.

"Did you know her? Gabriella?" She switched the spool of fabric to her right shoulder again. It was not super heavy, but it was awkward to hold.

"Why yes I did! She used to come into my shop almost every day. Sometimes multiple times a day! She was in the process of something grand before she passed away. It is very sad that her designs will never see the light of day."

"Gabriella is my mother—or was, I suppose. I'm here in New York to finalize her estate and whatnot."

"Oh! You are Calliope then, aren't you? How amazing it is that you have stumbled in on my little shop! How fortuitous!" He seemingly just realized she was holding the massive bolt of fabric and quickly took it from her. "Ah, yes! I've had this fabric on hand for so many years! I actually think I had special ordered it for your mother, but sadly she never picked it up. I can't remember for certain, but it is definitely something your mother would have liked!"

He looked at her seriously now. She could feel herself blushing slightly under his steady gaze. She could only imagine she looked like absolute crap. She could still feel the aftermath of the mini-breakdown, though the tears were now dried on her cheeks. Her hair was most likely disheveled from her quick exit from the gallery and when she had collapsed after her reckless run. Actually, her knees were a little red and sore from her stumble outside in front of the little garden. "Oh jeez. I'm so sorry. I must look like a mess."

He smiled at her. "Oh no! I was just thinking about how very much you look like your mother."

Fully blushing now, she looked down at her shoes briefly before smiling at him. "Thanks. I seem to be getting that a lot here in New York. I don't see it myself, but I'll take your word for it. Thank you."

"So, what brings you in today? Did you find a receipt with our address in your mother's things? That would be a happy accident!"

"Oh no, I quite literally stumbled upon your shop! I was across the street when I saw the red fabric fluttering in the wind and made my way over. I'd really like to buy it, if that is okay?"

"Oh my! No! I will not be taking a single cent from you! You can have that fabric. It's been sitting here literally for years upon years. I feel like it was meant for you! Please take it as my gift. And feel free to come back for anything you need here. If I don't have whatever it is, I can most definitely order it for you."

She gasped softly. This was way too nice of him. "Oh no, I couldn't possibly! I know that organza is an expensive piece of fabric and there must be at least fifty yards of fabric rolled up in that spool!"

He smiled brightly. "Actually, I believe it's more like seventy-five, but as I've said, it's been here for so very long I honestly can't remember. Besides, it was out in my clearance bin. I had just put it outside actually. This was meant to be!"

"I can't honestly take this! Please let me purchase something."

He shrugged, then pointed over to the far wall where there were a litany of different zippers and buttons. "Have a look over there and see what speaks to you. If you are making something similar to what your mother was working on, I'm sure you will find something."

Nodding, she wandered over to the display hanging from the wall. There were all kinds of buttons, from regular round ones to all shapes and sizes.

To the side there was a little shelf that held a bin of random clearance items, and a slight sparkle caught her eye. She rummaged through the bin and found a little plastic bag that held more buttons. Inside were a grouping of silver star-shaped buttons.

She peeled open the top so she could shake one of the buttons out to inspect it further. They were heavy, obviously made from sterling silver or possibly even stainless steel. She could tell they were the shank-style buttons. The star was the major piece of the button, and it had a little stand with a hole on the back of it. This allowed the seamstress to attach them to whatever clothing item they were making.

Turning the little plastic bag over, the rest of the buttons tumbled out into her hand. There were thirteen in total. One of them had what appeared to be little crystals embedded into the star that shimmered when she twisted the shank between her pointer finger and thumb. It instantly reminded her of The Shoes and the stars on the bottom.

"Oh, these buttons are gorgeous! I will happily take them if that's okay?" She slipped them all back in the little baggie and brought them over to the register. After she set them on the little counter, she turned to look at what other items she may need.

"These buttons have been here for years as well!" He smiled serenely as he watched her make her way through the store. She found more muslin to make more patterns for the pants she always wore, and also some red silk that matched the organza perfectly.

She was at the back of the store digging through another one of his clearance bins when she heard the jingle jangle of the shop door. She paused for a moment, wondering why she had not heard the bell ring when she first entered, before being pulled out of her reverie.

"Calliope Aisling Morgan! What on earth are you doing here?! Derek called your father freaking out because you ran out of the gallery, who then called me because he does not have your number! What in the glittery heaven is going on?" She turned to see her FGM standing in a pink cherry blossom kimono with matching pajama pants. Or at least she thought it was. Aretha's normally glorious head of hair was absolutely bare. And she was wearing a pair of square black Chanel glasses. Calli only recognized her because of her voice.

"Aretha? Is that you?" She put down the green silk she was holding and walked quickly up to where Aretha was standing. "Wait, how do you even know my middle name? No one knows that except my aunt." She was still in a pair of pink heels, of course, but these had the pink fuzzy feathers that you would expect on a pair of fuzzy slippers. "Oh my gosh! I love your shoes!"

"Thanks! I had them specifically made for me, but that's not what we are here for! Why are you here? Why did you run away from the gallery and, more importantly, Derrick?!"

"He took me to go see my mother's photographs." She could feel her lips start to tremble as she thought about what transpired. *No. I am not going to cry again.*

"He what?!" She knew that Calli had not wanted to see them. "What is wrong with that man?!"

Calli sniffled and then shrugged. "It's okay, Aretha. He didn't know I didn't want to see them. It isn't his fault. I'm okay now. And I happily found this little fabric store. Look at this organza I found! It was sitting outside like it was waiting for me to come find it!" She walked over to where the shop owner had left the organza to show Aretha. "Speaking of this organza, where is the shop owner?" She looked around and could not see him anywhere. "Now where did he go?"

Aretha looked at her incredulously. "So, you had a mental break-down, and now you are just here...shopping?"

"Um...yes. I suppose I am."

Just then, the gentleman shuffled back up to the front of the shop with a stack of fabric in his hands. "Here, dear! These will be going along with you as well. I had these on hold for your mother. I believe it's extra fabric from the designs she was working on." He added the new fabric to the pile of organza.

"Oh, I don't think I'll need those. You've been WAY too nice already!"

Aretha put a hand on her hip and wagged her finger at her. "What are you talking about? Of course we need that fabric! We are going to be putting on a show, darling! You need to finish those wonderful dresses your mom made!"

"I know, but he's giving me all this great stuff for free, and I need to pay him for something!"

"Well, hurry up and find something. I think I parked illegally."

The shop owner cleared his throat and said, "Oh, don't worry. The police don't bother my customers. As long as you have parked in front of my store, you will be okay. I have an unspoken agreement with them. The police chief always comes in to have me alter his uniforms."

Aretha took a moment to really look at him. "Hello, sir! Have we met? You look very familiar…" She looked at him quizzically as though trying to place him.

"No, I don't think we have! How do you know Miss Calliope?" he asked as he placed the red organza and other fabric into some reusable totes with the shop logo on them.

"Why, I'm her Fairy God Mother of course! Miss Aretha Thierry at your service, sir!" She did the little flourish like she had done with Calli the first time they met. "I don't have my business cards with me because I left in a hurry, but I'm sure I'll be seeing you again! I'm sure we will need your services over the next week or so." She smiled brightly at him before turning back to Calli.

"Okay, dear, let's get your items packed up into Betty. And then you can tell me exactly what happened tonight. We need to have a little chat by the way. You cannot go running off in the middle of the city without telling anyone where you are going!" She looked at Calli pointedly and tsk-tsked at her.

Calli blushed and said, "I'm so sorry Aretha. I did mean to call you. I just got distracted by the red organza, and you came so quickly!" She paused and looked at her. "Wait, how did you even know where I was?"

"Your phone, silly! I found where you were with the Find my iPhone app. I swear, child, you need a technology makeover." Aretha shook her head. "Because your phone is an added line to my account, I have access to your location if I need to find you." She looked at her pointedly. "I'm just happy you are okay and not dead in a ditch somewhere!"

"I am sorry. I will promise not to go running off into the streets of New York again without letting you know in advance."

Aretha nodded, but Calli could tell she was still a little bit upset with her.

Calli turned to the shop owner. "I'd love to have that green silk I found. Will you let me buy it from you? Please?"

"Oh, of course! I would be most delighted to sell you that silk. Do you know what you will make with it?"

She laughed and shook her head. "I have no idea. But I'm sure something will make itself known to me."

They went over to the register and he rang up the green silk. Even the sounds it made when the buttons were pushed were beautiful. He put the green silk in the same tote bag that held the red organza. "This color is called Moroccan Green, by the way. Maybe that will help inspire you!"

He took the glasses hanging from the chain around his neck and placed them precariously on his nose. "Let's see here, there's a total of five yards. And it will be thirty dollars per yard...so that makes it a total of one hundred and fifty dollars. Tax would be like eleven dollars, so let's just call it an even one hundred and sixty dollars. Sound good?"

Calli smiled. "Of course! That's totally okay. Thank you." She reached into her purse to pull out the little cigarette case that held her cards. "I'm so sorry, but I only have my debit and credit cards. I don't ever really carry cash."

"That is fine!" He smiled at her, opening a drawer under the cash register and pulling out a tablet.

He gently took the debit card she offered to him. After he swiped it, he held out the iPad so she could input her pin for the purchase.

"Wow, that's pretty cool! I'll have to tell my aunt about it for our flower shop!"

He pushed a few buttons on the cash register, and the drawer popped open. Grabbing the receipt, he handed to her with a smile.

"It was lovely meeting you, Miss Calliope."

"Oh my gosh. I just realized you know my name, but I have no idea what to call you! What is your name sir?"

"My friends call me Tony. And since you are Gabriella's daughter, you must absolutely call me Tony!" He nodded.

"Of course! And you can call me Calli. You know, now that we are friends." She smiled at him again. "Thank you again for all the fabric and especially those little star buttons! I can't wait to use them."

He reached over the little table and took her hand in his. "It was a pleasure to meet you, Miss Calli. I hope you will come visit my shop again sometime very soon." He gave her hand a squeeze before letting it go.

"Oh, absolutely!" She smiled again at him. "Thank you again, Tony!"

Chapter 11

Aretha shot her a look as she stomped over to Betty. The top was down, and the streetlights made the shimmer in her paint job sparkle. Aretha carefully placed the two shopping bags on the backseat before shooting her another look.

Calli sighed. "I'm sorry, Aretha. I didn't intend on running out of the gallery like that. I honestly didn't. It was just so overwhelming seeing my mom in all those photos. I had never seen any of her work so it was a bit devastating for me."

Her FGM went over to the driver's side of the Cadillac and shook her head. "It's okay. I'm sorry I'm upset with you, but this isn't the little town you live in back in Oregon. You can't just go running around New York City without letting anyone know where you are going or what's going on."

"I know, I know. I'm sorry." She slid into the passenger seat quietly. "I had actually just got off the phone with my aunt and was walking back to the street when I saw the red organza fluttering in the wind. I was completely distracted by it. It was like when I saw the sparkling of the stars on the box that held The Shoes. I just had to go check it out."

Aretha chuckled as she got into the car. "I know what that is like. It's hard being a creative type because you can get distracted so easily. Remind me to take you to Times Square at night so you can see it all alight! I think that will inspire you. Just please let me know next time you have a creative moment so I don't worry too much about you."

"I will. Definitely."

Aretha turned to her and nodded. "Good." She started the car, and it came to life with a fierce growl before settling into a low purring. "Betty has liked all the outings lately. She doesn't get out as much anymore because the traffic is usually so horrendous or I can just zip on over to wherever I need to go. She's very happy you are here."

Calli thought using the word zip was a weird way to comment about the subway, but she had never been on a subway so it was not like she knew what that was like. "Aw yay, that makes me excited to hear."

"So, how was your outing with Derrick before he made the mistake of taking you to see your mom's images? I'm certain he has the hots for you."

Calli blushed. "Oh, it was great before I saw the pictures. We were holding hands, walking around the gallery and talking. It would have been a great first date I think." She frowned. "I should probably call him, huh? And my father, I guess." Her frown deepened.

"Yeah, that is probably a good idea. Your dad's number is already programmed in the phone, but I didn't have Derrick's number to plug in for you. I'm sure your dad can give you his number."

"Okay." She paused a moment before pulling out her phone and looking through the contact list. There weren't any entries for 'Dad' or 'Father', but there was one for 'Xander'. She tapped his name and put the phone up to her ear, listening. On the fourth ring, he finally picked up.

"Hello? Calli? Is this you? Oh my god I have been so worried. Please let it be you."

Wow. He actually does sound worried. Wow!

"Yes, it's me. I'm so sorry for worrying you. I didn't intend for this to happen."

"It's okay! I'm just happy you are okay! Is Aretha there with you?"

"Hello, darling!" Aretha yelled over the growling of Betty and the nighttime traffic. "I found your wayward daughter in a little fabric shop in freaking Murray Hill of all places. This girl can move, apparently, since the gallery was like a mile away! And she ran in freaking heels. Albeit, teeny baby heels, but heels nonetheless!"

She could hear her father sigh.

"Anyway. I'm fine. I'm safe. I'm in the car with Aretha now, and we are heading back to the apartment."

"Okay. Good." He paused awkwardly.

She nodded, then realized he obviously could not see her, so she said, "Yeah."

Another awkward pause.

"Oh, um... Can I have Derrick's number please? I'd like to call him and apologize for running out of the gallery like that."

"Sure. I'll text it to you."

"Okay, thanks."

"So uh, Calli, do you have plans for dinner tomorrow night? I was wondering if you'd like to come over, and I'll cook you dinner."

"No, no plans yet."

"Okay!" He sounded excited, which was strange for her because he had been so monotone when they were talking at dinner the other night. Like he was just going through the motions of what was expected of him. "I'll have the driver come pick you up around seven. Sound good?"

"Yes."

"Excellent! I'll see you tomorrow.... And Calli?"

"Yes?"

"I am very happy you are here."

She did not respond and hung up the phone. A moment or two later, she received two text messages—one with Derrick's contact information, and the other with his address.

Well, I suppose it's good to know where he lives. Maybe I'll send him a Christmas card or something this year. Or maybe not, seeing as I didn't even know he existed.

She tapped the contact information for Derrick and saved it to her contacts. After, she immediately called him.

After five rings, it went to voicemail. "Oh hey, Derrick. I'm so very sorry about running out of the gallery like that. I'll explain why next time I see you. I promise. Again, I'm sorry."

"He didn't answer, did he?" Aretha asked.

"No."

"He's probably still out looking for you."

"Probably."

Aretha reached over and squeezed her hand softly. "He'll understand once you explain it to him."

"I hope so, 'cause I really do like him so far." She smiled sadly at Aretha and squeezed her hand back.

After parking, they gathered the two bags from Tony's little fabric shop and made their way to the apartment.

There at the end of the hall, looking slightly more disheveled than a few hours ago, sat Derrick by her door.

"Hey there." She half smiled and kinda waved at him.

"There you are! I've been worried sick about you, Calli."

"I'm so sorry! I can explain everything."

Aretha handed her the bags that she was carrying and demurely bowed before heading into her own apartment. Calli was shocked at how quiet she had been.

"Here, let me take those." He stood up quickly and took the bags from her.

"Thanks." She fished in her purse for the star keyring, then unlocked and opened the door.

Fortunately, it looked like Aretha was able to get someone to get rid of the fake wall between the two apartments. It honestly did not look like there had ever been a wall there at all.

"Um...am I going crazy, or was there a wall there yesterday? Cause I swear there was a wall there earlier..." Derrick looked between her and the new opening.

"Oh, yeah. That was one of the exciting things that happened last night. My mom had mentioned that she had had two apartments in the letter she had left for me, but I had no idea what she was talking about, nor did her attorney. I discovered it last night when I fell through."

She carefully put the key fob back into the Chanel bag, set it on the kitchen counter, and walked over to the new entryway to the next apartment. "Here, I'll show you what I found. And we can set the new fabric I picked up there as well."

She kicked off the Vara pumps and placed them on the coffee table. "Do you want a coffee or anything?"

"Nah, I'm good. But thank you."

"Okay, let me show you what I found yesterday."

He followed her through the new entrance and into the second apartment. She led him over to where the empty workstations were so he could set the two totes on the table.

"So, apparently my mom was designing her own fashion line. See?" She walked over to where the mannequins stood and uncovered the dress that resembled a sweet pea.

She walked back over to where he was standing next to the work tables. "There's a few that aren't finished yet, so I'm going to finish them. Aretha and I want to do a show in honor of my mom. Speaking of my mom…"

She sighed and leaned with her back against the table crossing her arms. "The reason why I ran away from the gallery tonight was because I was NOT expecting to see any photos of my mom. I've actually never seen any of her photos. Ever."

A shocked expression crossed his face as he looked at her. She could tell he wanted to say something but was waiting for her to finish.

"So, yeah. It was completely unexpected. I mean, I know she was beautiful, and I obviously know she was a model. But for me, that wasn't who she was. To me she has always just been Mom, you know? And for whatever reason, I wanted to keep her as such."

She sighed and ran her fingers through her hair. She almost never touched her hair because of the curls. But she already looked disheveled so what was the harm? Plus, the drive back to the apartment probably only added to the frizziness of her hair.

"So, seeing her in all her modeling glory was more than a shock. It was unbelievable. She was astoundingly beautiful. I can't believe she gave all that up because of me." She could not stop her lip from trembling. She knew she was going to cry and tried to hold it in.

Derrick came over to her and rubbed both her arms with his hands. "Hey, it's okay. I'm sorry I sprung it on you like that. I should've asked first."

She nodded, trying to keep the tears from falling.

"Come here." He pulled her into his arms and wrapped them entirely around her. "I've got you, okay?"

She let herself cry, loudly and uncontrollably, for a few moments. Calli was not a crier. She typically could handle most things that life had thrown at her, but being in the city surrounded with all her mother's things was making it very, very hard not to cry.

After a deep breath, she pulled away gently. "I'll be right back, I'm gonna blow my nose…" She smiled meekly at him and went into the restroom.

She shut the door softly behind her and took another deep, shuddering breath before looking in the mirror. What was left of her mascara hung precariously on her lashes. The rest was combined with the streaks of tears running down her face. Her hair was more than a bit disheveled and definitely had seen better days since her time in New York had started.

She sighed and opened up the medicine cabinet, hoping that there would be something she could use to put her hair up. Thankfully, Aretha had stocked it with the basics of q-tips, tissues, some makeup-removing wipes, cotton pads, and hair ties.

She took a minute to clean herself up and put her hair up in a high ponytail. She still looked like she had been crying, but at least she was somewhat presentable.

"Hi." She smiled sheepishly at him as she walked back over to the main table he was leaning against.

"Hi." He said warmly to her. "So, you and Aretha are going to hold a show or something then?"

"Yeah, it seems like my mom was in the process of getting things ready for her first ever fashion show. Hence the dresses I showed you earlier. I had absolutely no idea. Neither did Aretha, and that's saying a lot considering she's a freaking Fairy God Mother and knows everything."

Derrick shot her a questioning gaze at the term 'Fairy God Mother', but did not ask anything.

"Aretha and I want to do a show in honor of my mother, but I don't know what I'm doing. I mean, I can finish altering them and make them presentable I guess. But hosting a fashion show? I have no idea how to do that."

Derrick chuckled and looked at her. "Seriously? You have Aretha! I think, out of anyone I've ever met, she will know what to do. And besides... She's your 'Fairy God Mother', right? Whatever that's supposed to mean." He chuckled again. "I can't believe those words actually came out of my mouth. Like what world are we living in now? I mean, there are actually Fairy God Mothers now?" He ran his hand through his hair.

"Oh, don't even get me started on *The Shoes*."

"The what? I mean, you do have a lot of shoes."

"No, not shoes. THE SHOES. Apparently, there's this magical pair of heels that means the next great fashion designer has arrived or something. I found them last night in here as well."

"Oh! Wow! Do you actually have those? I mean, can I see them? Those things are famous. Like epically famous."

"Wait. How do YOU know about The Shoes and I didn't? There's something really wrong with this whole situation."

He smiled demurely at her. "I mean, I am a fashion photographer. I don't just answer your father's beck and call. I have my own interests, and photography is my main one. Whenever I have a moment to myself, I'm working with models or designers. I normally photograph fashion week but took this time off so I could help you get acclimated to being in New York."

She blushed. "That was really nice of you."

He smiled and shrugged half-heartedly. "It's not a big deal. I was due for some time off anyway."

"Oh! So that means you actually know some models? Do you think any of them would be interested in walking in the show for my mom?" She clapped her hands in excitement. "Please say you do!"

He laughed wholeheartedly, and after catching his breath said, "Yes, I do. I'll give my contacts a call tomorrow and see who's interested. I don't think you will have a problem finding models though. Your mother was very much loved in the fashion industry, and many would jump at the chance to model some of her work."

"Oh, awesome! Thank you so much, Derrick!" She laughed and hugged him.

He returned the hug before pulling back a bit to look down at her. "You are welcome."

They shared an awkward, close moment before separating.

"Um so, uh, anyway... I should probably go. You've had a long night, and I'm sure you have a ton of stuff to do tomorrow."

She cleared her throat and nodded. "Oh! Just so you know I haven't run away again or anything, I am going over to my dad's place tomorrow night for dinner. He sounded really excited about it, so that's good I guess."

He reached over and took her hand in his, giving it a squeeze. "He really is excited to have you home. I know he's very standoffish, but just give him some time. He'll warm up to you." He let her hand go as he started to walk to the front door of her mother's apartment. It was weird to use the one in the work area for some reason. It did not feel quite right. "Oh, and just wait until you see some of your father's work. He's an amazing photographer. Seriously. Even his landscape work is astounding."

She walked with him to the door. "Thank you for tonight. I know it ended kind of 'meh', but it really did start out wonderfully." When she said 'meh', she even used the hand quotes.

She stood up on her tippie toes and leaned in to give him a kiss on the cheek. He smiled warmly at her.

"I'll call you tomorrow and let you know what models I've found for your show, okay?"

"Sounds good. Thank you again."

"You are welcome." He nodded his head and gave an imaginary tilt of a hat before striding out into the hallway.

Chapter 12

Waking the next morning, she realized she was absolutely starving. With everything that happened, she had completely forgotten to eat last night.

Calli slipped out of bed and put the new panda slippers on before padding into the kitchen. She remembered seeing a bread box on the counter next to the new coffee maker and she hoped there was actually bread in it.

Happily, there was a fresh loaf waiting for her. "Now, let's see if there's a toaster." she murmured to herself. Starting with the cabinets nearest to her, she opened them all to see what they held. She located the plates and bowls, the pots and pans, and then finally found all the kitchen gadgets, including what looked like a brand new toaster.

"Okay, let's see what else we have. Hopefully, we have some eggs or something."

She padded over to the refrigerator and opened the door. Inside, she found all the basics like milk, cheese, eggs, bacon, and even some cream cheese. Aretha hooked her up! There were even some fresh strawberries, blueberries, and raspberries that were perfect for breakfast.

She pulled out the eggs, bacon, and milk and placed them on the counter. She grabbed one of the smaller mixing bowls and some eggs.

"Ooh, cinnamon... I need some cinnamon."

She went over to the upper cabinet nearest the stovetop and opened it, hoping it would have the cinnamon and any other type of herb or seasoning she might need. She opened the cabinet door and found a litany of spices and every kind of seasoning she could imagine. As she was going through them all, she heard a knock on the door.

Using the peephole, she looked through and just saw a bouffant of blonde hair.

"Oh hey, Aretha! I was just making some French toast, would you like some?" She asked as she opened the door, smiling.

"Good morning, dear! No, I already ate this morning, but I might have some tea."

"Okies! I'm not an amazing cook anyway, but I can get by." She laughed as they walked back together to the kitchen.

"No worries!"

"What kind of tea would you like? I think I have all the different kinds here."

"Oh, some black tea with a bit of milk would be fabulous. We are going to need all the caffeine today!" Aretha was wearing a long sleeveless pink dress that had a sheer overlay with white polka dots on it. She cinched the dress together with a wide silver belt. Her hair was in the huge styled bouffant that she was beginning to think was Aretha's regular hairdo. This time she had pinned up one side with a large barrette that was made up of cherry blossoms on their branches. Calli could not quite see what shoes she was wearing, but she caught a flash of silver just under the hem of the dress.

She grabbed the little pod of black tea, placed it in the coffee machine, and went to go find a suitable cup. No plain-Jane coffee cups for Miss Aretha, no definitely not! She remembered seeing a tea set with roses on it.

"Ah, there you are!" She exclaimed happily as she found the tea set. She grabbed one of the cups and a matching saucer. They were a lovely white set with roses blooming all across the cups.

Quickly, she went over to the little coffee maker and placed the delicate tea cup under the little spigot before pushing the button.

"My dad invited me over to his place at seven tonight for dinner." When the tea was ready, she turned to the refrigerator and grabbed the milk. The milk was in one of those little half-gallon glass bottles that were frequent in Clover. She brought both over to Aretha. "Here you go! Let me grab you a spoon—one second."

"Thank you, dear." Aretha smiled as she sat on one of the stools next to the island in the kitchen. Her makeup was flawless, as always, and she had just a hint of silver around her eyes. Her lips had a silvery pink lip gloss that matched the entire look.

"Okies," she said sadly.

Calli let Aretha lead her to the floor-length mirror, but she did not look up right away. She did not want to see the beautiful dress looking less than it should on her.

"Oh, darling, look up! I promise it doesn't look bad on you! I swear!"

Calli looked up and gasped. The dress looked perfect on her and fit exactly as it should. The thin straps of the fabric even had the same design of the polka dots as the dress. It alternated between large and small dots. The silver belt went perfectly with the dress and helped make it not look like a sack of potatoes like before.

"Oh my gosh." She looked amazing, even though she still had the leftover makeup from last night on her face and her hair definitely needed to be washed.

"Indeed, dear! Now, I'll go pick out some jewelry. I called Gary over while you were changing. Go hop in the shower, and I'll let him in for you. And I'll pick out some shoes for you to wear!"

Chapter 13

When Gary arrived, he did something she was sure most makeup artists did not do: He took the time to make sure she knew how to apply the makeup herself. He simply stood by and watched her apply it at her mother's makeup table, giving her tips and tricks to make it easier. It was an amazing gift and was super helpful.

Calli reached over and took Gary's hands, squeezing them in hers. "I just wanted to say thank you for everything you've done for me. I would still be completely in the dark about makeup and even hair if it wasn't for you. You truly are the best Fairy God Mother a girl could have. Just don't tell Aretha I told you that." She laughed softly.

"Oh no, I would never do that. Now quit making me feel all the things and finish up. Aretha will back in here any minute." He leaned down and quickly kissed the top of her head. "If you tell any single person I did that, I'll kill you. And trust me when I say that when a Fairy God Mother makes something disappear, it stays disappeared." He gave her a secretive look before handing her one of the lip glosses from the makeup table.

She smiled. "Oh no, I definitely believe you. Your secret's safe with me." She took the lipgloss and squeezed his hand before turning back to the mirror.

As Gary had predicted, just as she was finished applying her lip gloss, Aretha came into the bedroom.

"I think I have found the perfect piece for you to wear tonight!" Aretha gleamed and handed her a necklace-sized jewelry box. "Open it!"

She gently took the velvety dark blue box and opened it slowly. Inside, nestled on the white plush velvet was a necklace made of white gold that was shaped in a 'Y'. Along the chain were six small dark blue stones, with an additional stone sitting where the necklace connected, in the center of the Y. At the end of the single strand hanging down below the rest, was a larger stone resting at the bottom tip of the Y.

"Oh, it's beautiful. What do you think the stones are?"

Aretha peeked over her shoulder, then gently took the necklace from her. She carefully held up the largest of the eight stones to the light. "Oh, definitely sapphire. I thought it would look wonderful with the dress you are wearing tonight." Handing the necklace back to Calli, she stepped behind her to hold up her hair. "Put it on, and don't you dawdle, dear. Your father's car will be here any minute to whisk you away!"

Calli smiled and took the necklace carefully. It was a beautifully delicate piece. She set it in place and made sure that the lock was closed before settling back to look at her reflection in the mirror.

A soft gasp slipped out. She could actually see it. After all these years of people telling her, she could finally agree. "I look just like my mom." She smiled up at both Gary and Aretha, tears welling in her eyes.

"Oh, no! Don't you dare start crying!" Aretha exclaimed. "We don't have time for that now, honey. Let's go get your shoes! I've got a surprise for you."

Calli grabbed a tissue and dabbed underneath her eyes. Gary had shown her the correct way of dabbing her eyes without smearing her makeup after she had accidentally stabbed herself in the eye with the eyeliner. Her eye was still a little red from her mishap, but it wasn't noticeable.

She quickly got up from the makeup table and ran into the living room. "I was thinking I'd wear the Pigalles again tonight. What do you think?"

Aretha was standing next to the coffee table with a plain white shoe box in her hands. "Oh no, dear, you will wear these I think!"

"Ooh, what are they?" she asked. She went over to Aretha and gently took the box.

"I think you will love them!" Aretha even did a little shimmy when she said love. Calli could not help but smile.

She carefully removed the lid and set it on the coffee table. Inside were two dust covers holding pairs of heels. Quickly, she removed the dust cover on the first pair of shoes.

"Wait…are these? Are these my Benedettos? They look BRAND-freaking-NEW!"

"Yes they are! I figured you couldn't go see your father and not wear those shoes! They were your mother's favorite pair after all!"

"Oh, they were? How did I not know that?" Calli hurriedly placed the shoes on her feet. "Oh, they are perfect! They fit even better than before! How is that possible?"

Aretha laughed, "Oh, I have my ways. And the shoe cobbler I know is amazing! He can fix anything and make it all look brand new."

Calli went over to the full-length mirror near the front door and took in her reflection. She really did look like her mom tonight. It was almost a little scary, but she shrugged it off. She was her mother's daughter, after all. Why not embrace it?

Her hair curled in soft spirals, framing her face. Her makeup was soft and natural, only bringing out the best of her features. The necklace accented her collar bone, and the sapphires matched perfectly with the blue of her dress.

"Alright, you two, I'm off to go see my father. Let's hope this time goes easier than the first time…." she said a little nervously as she went to grab the little Chanel purse that held her wallet and phone. "My dad's driver should be here any minute."

Gary and Aretha each gave her a hug. Aretha's was fully enveloping whereas Gary's was almost medical. She just chuckled quietly to herself as she walked out the door.

As she stood outside of her father's apartment, she tried to calm her nerves. She was not as nervous as during their first meeting but was still definitely anxious. She cleared her throat and straightened her dress and necklace before knocking on the door.

A moment or two later, the door opened. Xander had a shocked expression on his face when he saw her. "Gabriella?"

"No, it's me…Calli." She was smiling, but still slightly hesitant.

"What?" He gave himself a shake before. "Oh, I'm so sorry. Of course! Calli, please come in." He held the door open for her so she could step into the apartment.

"Hi. Thanks for having me over."

"Oh, of course! Any time you are in New York, you will need to come by and have dinner. Okay?"

"Okay." She nodded and smiled genuinely at him. Tonight he was wearing a dark grey v-neck shirt and black slacks. But his feet were completely bare.

"If you don't mind taking your shoes off? It's something I picked up from all my travels. I have a little shoe rack. Here, let me show you." They walked into a small entryway that had an entrance to the living room to the left and the entrance to the kitchen on the right. On the left hand side near the door was the little shoe stand that he pointed out. "There you go."

"Thank you." She took her heels off and set them in an open space on the top of the stand.

"This way please." Gesturing to the right, they walked into the kitchen together. On their left was cabinet space, the microwave, and the oven. The room then opened up into a huge space that held the rest of the kitchen and dining room. There was a large dark wood table with matching chairs and beautiful modern windows.

On the far corner, opposite the entry wall, sat a beautiful oriental box. It was a larger box, and it appeared to be made out of mother of pearl. It actually looked like it might fit on top of the ornate table she had in her entryway.

"I hope you don't mind, but I made spaghetti and meatballs. Oh and some breadsticks, of course! I also have a Caesar salad and some steamed green beans, and all the Parmesan cheese your heart desires!" He laughed. "If you are anything like your mom, you'll just have some Parmesan cheese, copious amounts of bread, and a side of spaghetti?"

Calli laughed, tearing her eyes away from the box. "Yeah, that sounds about right. I can't help it if I love bread and cheese, you know? I think everyone secretly does. They're just afraid to admit it."

"Yeah, Italian food was definitely your mom's favorite." He laughed at a memory she could almost imagine that was playing in his head. He gave himself another shake before saying, "The pasta should pretty much be done, just let me check it. You can go have a seat at the table if you want."

"Okay. You sure you don't want me to help bring the food in?"

"Ah no, of course not. Just go sit down, please."

She smiled at him. "Okay." She took one last long look at the oriental box and then went to the table to sit down.

The salad and green beans were already on the table and looked delicious. He had laid out the plates and silverware so she sat down at the corner nearest to the kitchen so she was still able to see her father.

"How are you liking New York now that you've been here more than a few days?"

"It's still a bit overwhelming, but I seem to be adapting well to it. I'll be excited to return home after we do the show." She took a moment to take in her surroundings. Across from the table was the kitchen. The white cabinets really stood out against the dark wood storage on the entryway wall.

On the opposite wall from where she was sitting was a huge floor-to-ceiling collage of different-sized black and white photographs. They ranged from landscapes to close-ups of flowers. They all had at least a little bit of nature in them. Her favorite was the image of a willow tree that was in the center.

"Wait, what did you say? Did you say you are doing a show? What for?"

"Oh! I'm so sorry, I completely forgot to tell you!" She was not used to telling anyone other than her aunt what was going on in her life so having so many more people to share information with was something new for her. "So apparently, my mom was designing her own fashion collection in a super secret apartment. Not even Aretha knew about it. And Aretha knows everything." She laughed again. "Nor did I! And I was living with her at the time…. Although, I was a kid so it was probably pretty easy to hide it from me. I think she'd go work in the secret apartment after I went to bed, to be honest. She could be pretty sneaky…." She chuckled. "Anyway, Aretha and I think it would be a great idea to hold a show in honor of my mom and to show off her designs. I really hope to make Mom proud."

She realized after a moment of awkward silence that not only was he not talking, but he wasn't doing anything at all. He was just standing there, still, watching her. "Oh, um…yeah, sorry. I guess I got excited." She laughed awkwardly.

He gave himself another shake. "Sorry about that. You just reminded me of your mom. She would always get so animated whenever she was talking about something she was really interested in—which, honestly, was all the time." He laughed softly. "I just forgot what I was doing for a second." He grabbed the spaghetti and meatballs, brought them over, and set them on the table.

"Oh, that looks wonderful. Thank you!"

"The pasta is already buttered," he said as he set the bowl down, teeming with spaghetti noodles. "I figured once again, if you are anything like your mom, you'd want butter." He smiled briefly at her. It was almost a sad smile.

"Did you guys make pasta often? It was definitely one of the most common meals we had growing up."

"We actually did. It tasted great and it was fast, cheap, and easy." He laughed. "When we first met, we were both just starting out so being cheap was always the top priority. Although, we did splurge every now and then."

Just then, the timer on the oven went off. "That'll be the breadsticks! I'll be right back, and then you can explain the *secret apartment*."

He went into the kitchen and grabbed some oven mitts, then proceeded to pull the breadsticks out of the oven. After moving them from the cooking tray into a bread bowl, he grabbed another smaller bowl and set it on the table. Inside was freshly grated parmesan cheese and a little spoon to dole it out with.

"Okay, dinner is served." He smiled bashfully and made a sweeping motion over their dinner before sitting down at the end next to her.

"This looks amazing. Seriously. Thank you so much for cooking for me. I really appreciate it."

"It's no problem," he said as he grabbed the pot with the pasta in it and took a huge serving of the spaghetti. "So, tell me about this secret apartment. What's that all about?"

She ate a quick bite before saying, "Apparently Mom had started designing her own fashion collection. Did you know she had any interest in doing something like that?"

"No. We never talked about our work. Honestly, we were more focused on spending time together. I didn't even know she knew how to sew."

"Yeah, me neither!" Calli grabbed one of the breadsticks and dipped the end of it in the spaghetti sauce before she bit into it. "Oh man, these breadsticks are so good!"

"Thank you!" He smiled sheepishly. "I can show you how to make them sometime if you want. They're a secret family recipe actually."

"I didn't know you were Italian. But with the name Verona, I guess I should've known."

He laughed again. "Yeah, it's a pretty popular name with other Italians, I guess. And then there's that whole play Shakespeare wrote."

Calli laughed. "Very true!"

He grabbed a breadstick of his own and dipped it in the sauce like she had done before taking a big bite. "Oh yeah. That's good."

"It definitely is! Anyway, Mom was in the middle or actually pretty close to being done with the designs, so the plan is for me to finish up the final touches, and Aretha is going to help me get a show together. Oh, and Derrick is going to help me find some models."

"So, you know how to sew too?"

"Yeah, I learned how to sew in home economics in school, and just stuck with it. Although, I do more of the everyday wear, whereas Mom does the fancy couture gowns. It'll be slightly out of my wheelhouse, but they are mostly done. It shouldn't take me more than a day or two to get them finished."

As she adjusted her position in the chair slightly, the overhead lights reflected against the mother of pearl box, catching her eye as it looked like the box was almost shimmering.

Xander cleared his throat. "You okay??" She hadn't realized he had been watching her. Apparently, she had been staring at the box for more than a few minutes.

He gestured to the ornate box currently sitting on the kitchen counter. "You've been eyeing that the whole night," he said, his face in all seriousness.

"Oh, was it that obvious? I'm so sorry, but it just reminds me of this ornate table in my mom's apartment. I think it matches actually. I bet the little feet on it would even line up with the empty spots on my table at home." She blushed as she spoke.

"That's actually for you. It has all the photos and little momentos from your mom's and my time together. I hope you will grow to love it as much as I do." He blushed ever so slightly. She was thinking he really did love her. "I was planning on giving it to you when you got here so we could go through it together, but it's—it just still hurts too much. I'm sorry."

She reached over and took his hand in hers. "It's okay. I understand. Truly."

He squeezed her hand and said, "You can take it home if you'd like. It's kind of heavy being covered in mother of pearl, and more than a little awkward to move around, but I think you'll love the moments captured inside."

Calli smiled and squeezed his hand again. "That sounds wonderful. Thank you."

They had finished dinner and were sitting around the table just talking. About her life, all of his travels. It was just exactly what they needed. Before long, they both realized it was almost ten o'clock.

"I guess I'd better be going. It was a wonderful night, and I really appreciate you making dinner. Maybe before I go home we can cook together? I really need to learn how to make those breadsticks because they are AH-*MAY*-ZING!" She said 'amazing' all sing-songy. She got up and waited for him to stand also.

He laughed as he stood. "Oh, yes! Of course. Just keep me posted about how your time is going. I know you'll have a ton of stuff going on with the upcoming show and everything. But we will make it work."

"Sounds good to me." She nodded, and then they walked together to the door.

"Thanks, Dad." She smiled shyly at him for a moment before giving him a huge hug. It was their first-ever hug and the first time she had called him Dad. And it was glorious. He hesitated initially before finally hugging her back.

"I'm so happy you finally came," he whispered.

"Me too."

Chapter 14

Calli woke the next morning filled with tons of energy and was thoroughly inspired after her dinner with her dad. She was so relieved it went well, and it actually felt like they were getting to know one another.

It was still pretty early in the morning—five a.m. to be exact—so she padded into the kitchen wearing her fuzzy slippers and sushi pajamas and went straight to the coffee machine. It still was not quite the same as her loose leaf tea and teapot, but it was better than nothing. Plus, it was super convenient.

She took her mug full of green tea in both hands and went into the workspace. She wandered around looking at everything, trying to find a notebook or something to write on. She needed to take inventory of what she had to work with before finishing anything.

Calli remembered seeing multiple hardbound sketchbooks on the two large tables in the center of the apartment, so she went over to inspect them. The first one that she grabbed was completely empty inside.

"Now...where do I find a pen or something to write with?" She asked herself as she scanned the area nearby. There was not anything on the tabletops, nor did there appear to be anything on the bookcases nearby. "What the heck, Mom. I know you have to have some kind of writing utensils in here."

She drummed her fingers against the desk, thinking, and realized it sounded hollow. Maybe there are drawers?

Stepping back to look more closely at the tables, she realized there was enough room from the top of the table to the apron underneath for a possible drawer. She could not feel any knobs or indents to open a drawer, so she pushed gently on the apron. It moved just a teensy bit, so she pushed a little harder and the drawer finally made a small click and complied, releasing outward with a long squeak.

As the drawer slid out, it revealed an assortment of different shades of colored pencils. "Oooh…" Eagerly, she went to the second drawer and pushed it open. This drawer held a variety of different pens and markers in every color and tip or nib size.

She squealed. "Oh man. This is very dangerous." But, of course, in the best possible way. The first drawer of the next table she opened held erasers, pencil sharpeners, and anything else an artist may need to create sketches and drawings.

Oh man, this stuff all looks brand new. That doesn't make any sense to me at all.

Opening the last drawer, she gasped softly. Not only had she found a variety of different-sized paper stacked in an open container, but there was another envelope with her name written on it. She instantly recognized the handwriting of her name.

Without a thought, she grabbed the letter and opened it carefully. In reality, she wanted to tear that envelope open with complete abandon, but she wanted to save all these little notes from her mom. So, she made sure to take her time opening it.

Inside, there was a business card and a handwritten note from her mom.

My Dearest Calliope,

I'm so happy you've found the studio. I know I shouldn't have kept it a secret from you all, especially you, but I am going to be honest. I was nervous and anxious that no one would understand my designs. So I decided to keep them a secret. Until now, that is.

I hope you are having a great time here in New York and that you and your father have met. I hope he gave you the keepsake box that goes with the entryway table in our apartment. I'm sure he didn't tell you the story of how I received the table and the keepsake box, but I will.

It was a year or so into our relationship, and he had to go on assignment in China. He brought them back and gave them to me on our first anniversary. It was the first major gift he ever gave me, and I absolutely adore both pieces.

Right before you were born, he had to leave again, but for a much longer assignment. The wars in the Middle East were in full swing, and he was required to go document it all. So I gifted him the box with all the keepsakes from our various times together.

I have also replaced all of my art supplies for you. If you are anything like the boisterous child I know now, you will absolutely use every single thing in the studio. The pens and markers should all still work, but if not, you can go see Tammy at Owlsley Art Supplies. I'll put a business card in the envelope too so you have the address.

I hope my pieces inspire you.

Please do with them what you wish. I know that if you ask Aretha, she will help you put on a show, but that's solely up to you.

I love you and miss you oh so terribly.

- Momma

Calli took a moment to wipe her eyes before looking at the business card. Maybe she would go check out this shop. One could honestly never have enough art supplies, and it would be nice to visit more places her mom used to frequent.

Opening the drawer to its full length, she looked over the different types of paper in the drawer. Some were the cheaper plain off-white sketch paper, whereas the others were the heavier weight paper. They varied in size from five by seven all the way up to eleven by fourteen.

She grabbed several sheets of sketch paper and one of the red markers. Red was definitely her color. Then, she got to work inventorying everything.

Calli was just about finished with the inventory of all the fabric when the smell of fresh coffee and some kind of pastry wafted by her. Her stomach immediately sounded its protest at being oh so very empty. She wrote down the last item, and set the stack of papers over on the table before wandering into her apartment.

Aretha was setting out a carafe of coffee and the pastries she had brought on the kitchen island. Calli cleared her throat before saying, "Hi, Aretha."

"Oh! Oh, Dear!" Aretha turned quickly and almost dropped the pastry she had been holding. "Where on earth did you come from? I swear you just shaved a few years off my life! Scaring me like that?!" She quickly set the pastry down and shook her finger at Calli.

"Sorry! I didn't mean to scare you. I've just been in the workroom taking inventory of everything there. I'm trying to figure out what needs to be done and if I will need to go to the store for supplies or anything. But it honestly looks like Mom took care of everything." She smiled happily, thinking of the newest letter her mother had left for her.

Aretha put her hands on her hips and shook her head. "Child. I swear you will be the death of me." Her outfit today was probably one of the most relaxed outfits she had seen her in yet. It was a simple light pink peasant-style dress. Her hair was in a low bun, and she had little tendrils of her hair pulled out to frame her face.

"Wait—are you wearing flats?" Calli looked at her dumbfounded.

"Yes, but these are the Chloe ballet flats. They match this dress perfectly. Besides, I knew we'd be in your mom's workroom. I'd be pulling my heels off after a few hours anyway, and those beauties deserve to be worn."

"They are really cute. I'll have to go get some I think."

"Oh, you definitely do. Actually, dear, we'll go shopping before you leave to go back home to Oregon. That way I can get you loaded up on some new shoes to wear."

Calli smiled brightly at her. "Absolutely!" She stood next to Aretha to look at the spread she'd laid out. "This all smells wonderful. What did you bring?"

We have some traditional croissants, a couple pain au chocolat, which are basically chocolate-filled croissants, and a variety of fruit-filled danishes. And then copious amounts of coffee. This little carafe is magic and never runs out."

"Wait. Really?"

Aretha laughed loudly, her eyes dancing. "Of course not! But if we run out, I can get one of my fledglings to go get some."

"Fledglings?"

"Baby Fairy God Mothers. We all have to start somewhere, you know."

Calli was waiting for Aretha to offer more information, but then the doorbell rang.

"Oh! That should be Gary. He's come over to help too."

She opened the door without peeking through the peephole, saying, "Hey, Gary, what's up with 'fledglings'? Aretha was talking about them, but…"

She let the sentence trail off as she realized it was not Gary but her father. "Oh, hi! Sorry, I thought you were Gary." She laughed and shrugged.

He was wearing a relaxed pair of jeans, a plain white button-up shirt, and a pair of black loafers. He was smiling from ear to ear and holding the ornate mother of pearl box. "I was going to have Andrew, my driver, bring it by, but I decided to drop it off myself instead."

"Oh, I'm glad! Come in, and please ignore my pajamas. I got up this morning and went straight to work. Aretha just got here and brought some breakfast pastries. Oh, and coffee too."

"It's quite alright about your outfit. That reminds me that we should go out for sushi sometime soon. Derrick and I know all the great sushi places. And I'll never say no to a good cup of coffee."

Calli chuckled as she led her father into the apartment. "Aretha updated the apartment for me before I came, so that was awesome. She's been really great while I've been here."

Aretha was sitting on the sofa with her laptop in her lap. "My ears are burning. What are you and Gary talking about me for?"

"Aretha…" They stopped in front of her and Calli waited until she looked up. "Aretha, this is my dad, Alexander Verona." It was just the second time she had called him dad.

Aretha made a surprised 'O' with her mouth a moment before setting the laptop on the coffee table and standing up. "Hello, Mr. Verona. It's a pleasure to finally meet you." She smiled demurely and curtseyed.

"The pleasure is all mine! And you can call me Xander. All my friends do."

Calli stood there a moment watching this all transpire. *Did I wake up in some weird alternate universe or something? Why is she acting so demurely toward him?*

Her father turned toward Calli and asked, "Where should I set this? It's not too heavy, but it's starting to get less and less light." He chuckled again.

"You can set it on the coffee table. I'll look at it all later tonight. We've got a lot to do, I think, in order to get this show ready. I honestly don't even know what we need to do." She frowned and looked at Aretha. "I have no idea what I'm doing."

"Honey, don't you worry your pretty little head about that. That's what Fairy God Mothers are for."

Xander looked between the two of them but just smiled. "Well, I will let you ladies get to it. I'll give Derrick all my contacts in the fashion industry, just in case you need them. He actually has quite a few himself, so I think you will be all set."

"Thanks, Dad." Saying it again made her smile. It did not even sound weird to her anymore.

"You are most welcome, Calli. You have my cell number now, so please call me if you need anything, okay?"

"I will. Thanks again."

Chapter 15

Gary arrived a few minutes after her father left. After they had eaten their fill of pastries, they went into the studio apartment to get to work.

Calli hadn't had a chance to go through the bookshelves and complete an inventory list of the items there, so that was assigned to Gary. Aretha took it upon herself to get the fabric and extra bits that Tony had given them the other night sorted based on the dresses they matched with so Calli would not have to go searching for the items. She even went through the inventory lists Calli had made and grabbed any essential items she thought that Calli would need to complete the dresses.

Calli quickly looked over each of the dresses and made notes of what to tweak on each in the sketchbook her mother had left for her. Luckily, most of them only needed a few adjustments here and there. And once she had the models' measurements, she would be able to get them finished for the show.

Her biggest task, however, would be the two rose-themed dresses. The two corset tops were already finished, but the skirts were sadly nowhere near where they needed to be. Her mother had placed all the panels for the rose petals, but they were not sewn to the main garment, nor were they hemmed.

So, that was where she started—first, hemming all the different panels for the petals, and then she slowly began attaching them carefully to the skirt of the dress. It was tedious work, but after a few hours, she had finally attached the final petal to the white rose dress. She took a step back to look over her work.

The dress was so simple yet absolutely breathtaking. Her amazing mom had been able to figure out a way to sew the petals in a way that made them voluminous and full. Just like a real rose petal would be.

Calli spun the mannequin so that the skirt would flare out to its full potential.

"It's astounding, Calli. Really."

She turned and found Aretha and Gary standing a few feet behind her. Calli looked between the two of them and the dress.

"You really think so? I'm a little out of practice, but Mom had it all laid out for me pretty much, so it wasn't too bad." *Thank you, Mom.*

"Really. It's beautiful, dear." Aretha smiled. "Your mom would definitely be proud."

"Thanks, Aretha."

"You're welcome, dear. Now come have a look at what Gary found! I think this will help you."

Gary led her over to the workstations. On the table opposite to the stack of sketchbooks, there was now a very large cork board.

"What is this?" She asked as she walked up to inspect it in more detail.

"I found it behind the bookcases. I think it had been hanging above them but fell down at some point. I only realized it was there because I knocked one of the smaller books off the top and it fell behind. You were so engrossed in what you were doing that we decided to put it here until you were finished."

"Thanks, Gary." She smiled at him before turning to fully take in all the details of the corkboard.

It was roughly thirty inches long by twenty inches tall, and it was covered in all sorts of items. It took Calli a moment to realize there was a method to the madness pinned to the board, reminding her of her aunt's areas in the flower shop.

There were several color images of the various flowers used for her mother's collection. Each flower had at least two if not more images posted in a clump, and surrounding each of the images were fabric samples, actual dried versions of the flowers, and five-by-seven sketches of each dress.

"Ooh, this must be her mood board," Calli said.

"Oh yes, darling. That must be what it is. Honestly, my entire apartment is just one bright mood board." Aretha laughed.

In the center were several images of peonies, including a smaller version of the same image Calli had hanging above her bed back in Oregon. But there were just the images of the peonies, no fabric swatches or sketches to go with them. "It looks like she was possibly starting to work on a peony-themed dress next. Too bad there's no sketches or anything. Hmm..."

"Hmm, what?" Aretha asked as placed her hands on her hips.

"Oh, nothing. I was just thinking it would have been really cool if she had started the peony dress so I could finish it, that's all. Peonies are her, my aunt's, and my favorite flower after all. It's a shame really."

She turned toward Aretha and Gary and caught the look that passed between them. "What?"

"Well, you seem to be doing so well on your own. Couldn't you design it yourself? You said you made your own clothes," Aretha said.

"Making a shirt and pants is COMPLETELY different than making an avant-garde dress. There's a million more steps, and I wouldn't even know where to start, honestly. It's a nice idea though. Mom would've loved it."

Aretha and Gary shared another look but didn't say anything.

"I'm starving. How about we order a pizza while I work on the red rose dress? It shouldn't take me nearly as long as the white one because now I know what I'm doing." She chuckled.

"I'll take care of the pizza. And I know just the place! One of the Fairy God Mothers owns a pizza joint that's pretty close." Aretha smiled.

"Wait, Fairy God Mothers also own pizza shops?"

"Of course! Fairy God Mothers are in every industry in the world. We aren't just for fashionistas and makeup fans. Come on, girl. This is the twenty-first century!"

Calli laughed. "Yeah, I guess that makes sense."

"Plus, it'll be the best pizza you have EVER had. I promise."

"That sounds great! Thank you, Aretha."

Calli was a third of the way through with finishing the red rose dress when the pizza arrived. Aretha had left to go grab the pizza from the delivery person when there was a commotion by the door.

"Darling! It is so great to see you! You didn't need to deliver this yourself, you know!"

"And miss the chance of meeting your protégé?! Absolutely not!"

Calli quickly finished the petal she was working on before turning off the sewing machine and going to see what was going on. There in the entryway stood a younger woman dressed in all black. Even the Vans shoes she was wearing were completely black, including the laces.

"Hi! Thanks for bringing the pizza over. It smells amazing!" Calli said as she walked over and extended her hand. "I'm Calli," she added, shaking hands.

She smiled. "I'm Kayla Aine. Sorry about not sending one of my delivery people, but when Aretha mentioned who the pizza was for, I had to come over myself!" She laughed. Her blonde hair fell just below her shoulders, and her green eyes danced as she laughed.

"It's nice to meet you! Anyone that loves pizza as much as me is definitely a friend of mine! Although, can I be honest? When Aretha mentioned she knew a Fairy God Mother that owned a pizza shop, I was kind of expecting an older Italian guy or something."

Kayla really laughed then, a full belly laugh that even made Calli giggle.

"I'm sorry, was that wrong of me to say?" She looked between Aretha and Kayla.

"Oh no, of course not. I hear it all the time," she replied after she caught her breath from laughing. "It shouldn't still tickle me this way five years in, but it still does."

Aretha looked between the two of them and said, "All right, chickadees, let's move this into the kitchen. I am starving, and I know that Gary is surely wilting away waiting."

"Oh, let's not keep Gary waiting!" Kayla said and happily marched into the kitchen.

Aretha set the five pizza boxes on the island and grabbed some plates. Gary wandered in from the workroom and immediately went to the pizza boxes, opening each one and setting them in a line to inspect the contents.

Kayla pointed at each box as she said what they held inside. "Here we have the traditional Margherita style, the Neapolitan, a classic pepperoni, a classic cheese, and one of my own design!"

"Oh, these look amazing!" Calli said as she went to look in each box. Aretha and Gary had already grabbed a slice of each one, so Calli followed suit. Making a neat little stack of pizza slices on her plate, she started with the heavier ones first, leaving the cheese for the very top.

Calli ended up leaning against the counter because she was absolutely ravenous and took a bite of the cheese pizza. The flavors exploded in her mouth. The richness of the tomatoes and the creaminess of the different cheeses. She could tell there was not just mozzarella.

"Oh my god. This may actually be the absolute best pizza I have ever eaten. Oh man." She quickly devoured the rest of the slice before biting into the pepperoni.

"Wait. I changed my mind. This one is actually the best!"

Kayla laughed. "Oh, just wait until you taste my special custom one. It's almost better than sex, but please don't tell my wife that." She laughed again.

"Seriously though! I've never had pizza like this. It's amazing!"

"Thanks! I actually am a trained chef. I graduated from Cordon Bleu in Italy and have a three-year bachelor's degree from there, but I fell in love with the way they make traditional artisan pizza and have never looked back."

She leaned over and whispered, "It's all about the crust, you know. They use sourdough bread for the crust, and that adds SO much flavor. Plus, we use a brick oven so that adds to every single bite. The type of wood used will add or subtract in various ways. It's amazing how much of a difference a piece of pecan wood does versus a piece of hickory. It's incredible."

"Oh! Is that what it is?"

Aretha cleared her throat and said matter of factly, "It's also the water. Did you know there are pizza companies that started in New York City that have branched out to other cities and states that purposely transport the water from here to wherever they are? It's supposedly the mix of minerals that give New York pies their texture and flavor."

"Wait. Seriously? They love the tap water so much they get it delivered out of state? That's a little weird but...I mean, I think this is the most perfect slice I've ever had, so I guess that makes sense."

"That and always using the best and freshest ingredients. Being a Fairy God Mother does have its perks."

"I'm so sorry, but I just don't see it. I thought you'd be more dressed up or something." Calli laughed awkwardly.

Kayla smiled. "Do you know how badly the pizza sauce stains? There's no way I would wear anything other than black when I'm working. And I'll have to retire these plain black clothes pretty quickly because even they fade and get stained. But it's all about the sauce. And the crust and the cheese!" She laughed again.

"Oh, I definitely agree," Calli reiterated as she took another bite of the Neapolitan slice.

Kayla nudged Aretha. "And she hasn't even had my custom one yet."

"Hold on, I can only eat so fast." Calli said around the last bite.

To say it was absolutely amazing would be an understatement. It was beyond anything she had ever eaten. "Okay, I was completely wrong about what I said earlier." She managed to get out in between bites. "This slice here is the most astounding food item I have ever eaten. Please, please tell me what's in it."

"Well, it starts with the cheese. This little beauty has mozzarella AND goat cheese! That's why it's so creamy and smokey at the same time. Then we have some grape tomatoes to give it that little pop as you're eating it. Add some mushrooms, green and black olives, Italian sausage, and then it's drizzled with the balsamic vinegar. And, technically, there's no sauce because we use an olive oil base."

"Ah lub if..." Calli gushed through a mouthful of pizza.

"What, dear?" Aretha asked. She and Gary had finished their pizza and were currently sitting on the couch.

Calli finally swallowed and repeated, "I love it. Seriously. I will never order another pizza from another shop. Ever. I may actually move here permanently just for this pizza right here."

Aretha and Gary both laughed. "See, Gary? I told you Kayla's pizza would do the trick."

Gary just nodded and smiled.

"I need to know the name of your shop, please. And don't be surprised if we order from you frequently!"

"I'll tell you if you give me a sneak peek at what you've got going in the other room! I know I don't look like it, but I love fashion and am so excited to see your mother's designs. I'm sad I never met her, but seeing her designs will be amazing. I was always such a big fan."

"Of course! Just let me devour another slice of that magical pizza and then I'll give you a little tour." She smiled before folding the slice of pizza in half so she could consume it quicker.

A moment or so later, she accompanied Kayla into the other apartment and showed her all of her mother's designs. Kayla's favorite was the white rose dress that she had just finished.

"It really does remind me of roses! That's crazy how you were able to do that!"

"Well, it's my mom's design. I just executed it."

"And you executed it perfectly. Seriously. If I ever need a dress or anything, I'm coming to you!"

Aretha called from the other room. "If you ignore the sushi pajamas she's wearing right now, she actually does tailor wonderful pants. Maybe you could get her to design some uniforms for your pizza shop."

"Yes! Let's do that soon!" Kayla exclaimed. "Obviously, after your show. Do you know when it's going to be yet? Or where?"

"No, not yet, but we are getting close, I think. Aretha put out some feelers for locations, and my friend Derrick is a photographer and has connections with different models, so I should find out more soon. Here! Let me write down your number and I'll call you when I know more, okay?"

"Actually, here, you can have one of my business cards." She reached into her back pocket and Calli could swear she saw a flash of bright red before she handed her a simple white business card. It had the name of Kayla's shop "Wingin' It Pizza", as well as the addresses of four different locations. On the other side was an adorable logo of an open pizza box with fairy wings.

"Did I just see something sparkle?"

"Oh, of course not!" replied Aretha as she walked in with someone following right behind. "You have a visitor, dear," she said as she stepped out of the doorway to reveal Derrick.

"Oh, crap." She was still wearing her sushi pajamas, and she was pretty sure she had spilled some of the pizza sauce on her shirt.

Derrick just smiled and said, "I like your pajamas. Much better than that 'I love New York' t-shirt you had on the last time I came over unannounced." He chuckled with the memory.

"Please excuse me for a moment! I'll be right back." She ran out to change. She grabbed her pants and the t-shirt she had worn her first day here.

When she came back, she found Derrick chowing down on a piece of that amazing pizza, with Kayla, Aretha, and Gary chatting around him.

"I'm sorry I was still in my pajamas, but I woke up and just started working on everything. I was inspired..." She shrugged softly.

"It's alright, dear! Derrick was just telling us about the models he found for you."

Derrick swallowed the last mouthful of pizza and cleared his throat before saying, "Yeah, we should be good. All the models I know are beyond excited about this show. You see, they all told their model friends, who told their model friends, and so on. So, I don't think we will have any shortage of models."

"Yay! That's great news. Thank you, Derrick. When can I meet them all?"

"I wanted to double check with you, but could they all come over tomorrow evening? Or even tonight?"

"Well, tonight I have to finish making the alterations on all the dresses here and finish the red rose dress. I think tomorrow will be better."

"Okay, no problem! Give me a few and I'll call the models I contacted so they can help spread the word. We will do it here, correct?"

"Yes, I think that makes the most sense."

Derrick nodded and walked over toward the windows to make his calls.

Chapter 16

Calli finished the red rose dress and spun it around so the petals unfurled softly.

"Oh, the movement of it is amazing, Calli. Really," Gary commented as it spun. "Did you know roses are my favorite flower? Red ones especially."

"No, I didn't, Gary. Thanks for letting me know."

"Pink flowers, in general, are my favorite, but I lean toward the bigger ones, like ranunculus hydrangea or dahlias. But peonies are one of my top five. I honestly love all the flowers. I mean, how can you not?" Aretha mused.

"Why does that not surprise me?" Calli asked, laughing.

"So, what's the plan for the rest of the day?" Derrick asked.

"Well, I need to finish up the other nine dresses, but it shouldn't take me very long. Why?"

"I was going to see if you wanted to go get dinner. Do you like burgers by any chance? I know of this great hole in the wall place called All the Fixins that has the most amazing burgers ever. And their French fries are out of this world. Hands down, the best fries I've ever had. Especially if you get the cheesy bacon truffle ones." He closed his eyes in pure bliss.

"Well, that definitely sounds like a place I have to go to. Also, I love burgers. I will never say no to pizza, burgers, or Italian food. Those are my absolute favorites."

"Well, if it's okay with you, Gary and I are going to go see one of our colleagues. She is starring in *Wicked*, and we are so excited for her. It's her first big show, actually." Aretha and Gary shared another one of their many looks, which made Calli not entirely believe that they had not planned this out in advance.

"Okay, well, thank you for all your help today. I couldn't have done it all without you. Well, I mean, I could, but it would be like a hundred days later or something. Anyway, thank you."

"You are welcome, dear. That's what Fairy God Mothers are for, after all."

Derrick just quirked his eyebrows at Calli and shook his head.

"Okay. You were right. The food here is legit amazing," Calli said through a mouthful of fries.

Derrick laughed and took a big bite of his own burger. A moment later, he said, "It really is the best burger joint around."

"Thanks for bringing me here. This is officially my most favorite place ever." He was sitting across from her at the little table so she leaned over and mockingly whispered, "Do you think the shakes are as amazing as the burgers?"

"Oh, definitely. They are on a whole other level." He smiled as she leaned back in her seat and then leaned over to mock-whisper back, "They are gigantic though, so maybe we should share one?"

She blushed and then stammered out. "Oh—okay."

He laughed and leaned back in his seat. "So, based on your love of tea, I was thinking we'd order one of their green tea matcha shakes. It's amazing. And, as an added bonus, they pile on a bunch of matcha-flavored macarons. It's one of my favorites."

"That sounds great." She smiled. It was nice that he remembered her love of tea. It was definitely her drink of choice.

She cleared her throat. "So, tell me about yourself. I feel like you know so much about me, but to me you're this dark mysterious figure that came out to bring me here. I know you are a photographer and love Roland Arsenault, but that's about it." She laughed. "Oh, I forgot! You used to have a pretty serious cell phone addiction, but that seems to have subsided."

At least when you are with me. And that made her happy.

He laughed again. "I'm never going to live that down, am I?"

"Nope. Never."

"Alrighty then, let me order the Matcha Madness shake, and then I will reveal more. Deal?"

"Deal." She nodded and sat back into her seat to watch him interact with the waitress. He was incredibly polite and even made the waitress laugh.

After the order was placed, he turned his focus back on her and was caught a little off guard when he realized she was watching him and not devouring more of her food.

"Wait. Are YOU blushing?" she asked, shocked.

He nervously rubbed the back of his head. "Yeah, I guess I am." He shrugged then. "So, I grew up in Massachusetts. I have a younger sister named Eliza, and she lives back in Mass. My mom actually lives next door to my sister, so that's pretty cool. I have no idea about my father. I apparently met him once when we were young, but I don't remember anything about him. He and my mom got divorced shortly after my sister was born."

"Ah, so we have the absentee father thing in common."

"Yeah, apparently. Although, it seems like Xander wants to be more involved now, so that's good. I want nothing to do with my father. Honestly."

"I get that. Trust me. But it has been nice getting to know him. He seems like a good guy."

"Oh, he is. He does a ton of work for various charities and non-profits. And every year he releases never-before-seen photos from his time during the various wars and auctions them off. One hundred per-cent of the funds from the auction go to a charity in the country the picture was taken. It's pretty amazing."

"That sounds incredible. I had no idea."

He reached over and took her hand in his. "He's done some really incredible things in his life. You should ask him about them. Or you could always Google him. He hates it when people say they learned about him from the internet." He laughed and squeezed her hand.

"I will once we get this show finished. I don't even know what day it is anymore." She laughed and squeezed his hand back.

They sat for a few moments just holding hands until the waitress brought up the check and the green tea shake. To say it was massive is an understatement. Somehow, in her mind, even though Derrick had said it was gigantic, she was thinking it would still be an average size. Nope. This shake was enormous.

The green tea shake itself was in a giant mason jar that had two bright neon green and white striped straws barely peeking out of the top—barely. Because, even though the straws themselves were also gigantic, the toppings covered almost the entire straw.

"This is...wow. It's huge!" She laughed. "I don't think we are going to be able to eat it all."

"See? I told you! The best part is the matcha whipped cream. They actually use the same matcha powder that they use in the shake and make their own matcha-flavored whipped cream."

The shake itself was the bright green from the matcha powder and they had rimmed the glass with matcha powder as well. The whipped cream alternated between a level of the normal flavor and then of the green tea whipped cream. Placed around the tower of whipped cream were the matcha macarons. There were ten in total.

"Is it bad that I want to just stick my face in it?"

Derrick laughed wholeheartedly. "Absolutely understandable, but please don't. I want to eat it too." He squeezed her hand. She just realized they were still holding hands. It felt so natural. "Let's dig into this, shall we?"

"We shall. Oh hey, you've got some ketchup on your face."

"What? Where?" He grabbed his napkin and swiped it over his face.

"You just missed it. Here let me help." She smiled innocently as she quickly swiped her finger in the green and white whipped cream, and then rubbed it on his nose.

"Oh man. You are lucky we are out in public or you'd have a nice-sized whipped cream dollop on your face. Maybe even with one of these macarons." He mumbled from behind the napkin as he wiped the whipped cream from his nose.

She giggled. "I will be forever vigilant in preventing any shenanigans like that from happening."

"Challenge accepted."

She grabbed one of the many macarons and took a bite. The flavor from the green tea exploded in her mouth, then she could taste the vanilla from the buttercream filling. "Oh, wow."

"Yep. Now try the actual shake."

She finished eating the macaron and slid the mason jar closer so she could take a sip. The moment it hit her tongue, she had to close her eyes to savor the flavors. Immediately, she took another sip, her eyes still closed.

"I may get brain freeze if I keep going, so here, have some," she said as she slid the shake closer to him. She did, however, steal another one of the macarons to devour.

"Thanks. I'm happy you like it," he said in between sips.

"I may have to move here if only to be able to partake in all of the amazing restaurants. I'm sure this place isn't the only place you love here."

He smiled and ate one of the macrons before he said, "I will definitely be your tour guide. If you ever do decide to move, that is." He slid the shake back over to her side. "Your turn."

"Yay!" She laughed as she took another big sip. The creamy texture of the shake itself blended so well with the flavor of the matcha. It was like a match made in heaven with a hint of something sweet in the actual shake.

"Do they make it with vanilla ice cream?" She asked as she grabbed another of the macarons and used it to scoop up a huge portion of the whipped cream.

"Oh, definitely. They actually get the ice cream from a local shop. Same with the macarons. They are from the bakery across the street."

"Really? That's awesome."

"Yeah, that's one of the reasons I like coming here. I'd much rather support a local business versus some huge corporation."

"I get that. I'm pretty much the same, actually, but it's easier back in Clover. We have some corporations, like the traditional restaurants and corner stores, but it's mostly locally owned shops. We don't even have a Walmart."

"That's funny. New York City doesn't even have any Walmarts. Like, at all. The nearest ones are in New Jersey, and one in Valley Stream, New York."

"Wait what? New York City doesn't have a Walmart?"

"Yeah, they've been trying for years, and any time there's a potential new store opening up, the people in the area pretty much riot. New York City is known for supporting mom and pop stores. It's one of the reasons I love it here."

"That's so cool. I never knew that about the city." She dipped her finger in the whipped cream and then along the side of the glass to pick up some of the matcha on the rim. "So, besides being a regular supporter of the individually owned shops, what else are you into?"

"I watch wrestling." He shrugged. "It's one of my guilty pleasures."

"Wrestling? Like Olympic-style wrestling?"

"What? No... No." He shook his head. "I mean wrestling, like what the Rock used to do before he got into Hollywood and started acting professionally. You know, Monday Night Raw?"

"I mean, I know of it, but I've never actually watched it. It's all fake isn't it?"

Derrick sighed and put his head in his hands a moment before looking at her seriously. "I'm sure there are younger fans that don't realize it's all choreographed, but it's basically the same as movies or TV shows. Yes, everything is choreographed, but the amount of work the people put into their characters and the physical fitness is amazing. It's like a violent floor gymnastics routine. The athleticism is astounding. We will have to watch some. After your show, of course."

"Of course." She reached over and took his hand in hers. "Thank you for bringing me here and introducing me to this amazing milkshake. I, however, think I'm in a food-coma now." She laughed and squeezed his hand.

He squeezed her hand, then brought it up to kiss it. "It's my pleasure, my lady." He blinked. "Sorry, that sounded weird."

She laughed. "Yeah, let's never call me 'my lady' again, please. I just had a mental image of you dressed up in an outfit like what they wore in the 1800s. Not that that's a bad thing or anything, but it just doesn't really fit with your whole...look? I guess? Anyway, I'm just rambling now." She laughed awkwardly. "Can I have my hand back? I guess you can keep holding it like that if you want, but it is weird."

"Yeah, sorry. I guess I short-circuited there for a moment." He laughed and set her hand back on the table but still holding it.

"So, what's the plan for tomorrow? What time is everyone coming over?"

"I've invited all the models to come over at one so you can meet them all and see which ones you'd like to have in the show. There were eleven total dresses, correct?"

"Yes, eleven. Why?"

"You will have your pick of the models. I think we will have about twenty show up."

"Wow! Really? That's kind of cool."

"Well, they all started talking, and as soon as word got out about your mother's dresses, it spread like wildfire." He shrugged, still not letting go of her hand. "Your mother had a huge following when she was alive, so this doesn't surprise me at all."

"Well, thank you. I'm excited to meet everyone."

"It's gonna be fun." He looked down at the table, surveying the damage they had done to their food. "Are you ready to go back to your mom's apartment? We've pretty much demolished everything here." He chuckled.

"Yeah, let's go. I'm so full I may actually explode if I move too fast." She squeezed his hand. "Do you want to split the bill? Or I can pay for it. I don't mind."

"Oh no, I've got it. It's my treat." He squeezed her hand again before letting it go so he could grab his wallet. He pulled out enough cash to cover the bill and left a significant amount for a tip. Her aunt had always said never date a man who does not tip well, and she had always kept that in mind with the few people she had dated.

"Thank you. Tonight was great."

"Agreed."

They walked home from the restaurant, hand in hand. They talked more about his life and how he started out as a photographer. His great-grandfather had left him an old Rolleiflex camera when he was a kid, and that had started his obsession with photography.

"I still have it, you know," he said as they walked up to her apartment door.

"Your great-grandfather's camera? I am not surprised at all. I mean, I still have all my mother's shoes." She laughed softly.

Derrick chuckled. "Remind me to show you sometime. I even have the first pictures I ever took."

"Oooh, I'd love to see them."

"You know, you are going to need to stay here for a couple weeks after the show because of all the stuff we want to do together."

Before you go home. She thought it to herself. It was becoming a negative now, her leaving to go home. If you had asked her a few days ago, she would have resoundingly said she could not wait to go home. Now? Not so much.

She took both of his hands in hers and squeezed them. "Thanks again for the amazing food and the incredibly great company tonight. It was just what I needed."

"You are welcome." He slipped one of his hands free from hers so he could tuck a wayward curl behind her ear. "I really had a great night. Like epically great. I definitely want to do this again sometime soon."

"Yes, please." She stood up on her tiptoes and kissed his cheek. "Goodnight, Derrick. I'll see you tomorrow."

"Yes, tomorrow." He tipped his imaginary hat to her again and headed toward the elevator.

Chapter 17

Calli leaned against the front door of the apartment for a moment, closing her eyes. "This is definitely not part of the plan…" she muttered under her breath. This was just supposed to be a quick trip to New York, but she was developing feelings for Derrick. Pretty quickly to be exact.

Letting a frustrated sigh slip out, she ran her hands through her hair. It was too late in the evening to start working on the last of the dresses, but it was still too early to go to bed. Sighing again, she entered the apartment.

As she walked into the living room, her eyes were immediately drawn to the mother of pearl box her father had brought to her this morning. She could just imagine what kind of interesting goodies were in there. And looking through the box would keep her distracted and not thinking of other things—like Derrick and her growing feelings for him.

Okay, Mom, looks like you, me, and Dad are going to go on a little trip down memory lane. This should be fun!

"I'll be right back," she said to the box before running into her bedroom to change into her sushi pajamas. A moment later, she ran back into the living room to grab the box. It definitely was heavier than she expected, and she could hear some of the items inside shift as she walked into her mother's room.

She had not slept in her mother's bed since arriving, but it just felt right to open the memory box there, surrounded by her things. Placing the box gently on the bed, she said, "Okay, one second. I just want to get some tea and then we will see what all you have inside." She did not know why she was talking to the box like she was, but it just felt… right. She patted the top of the box lovingly before she darted back into the kitchen for her tea.

A few minutes later, she was back in the room with her tea and set it on the nightstand. She was sure Aretha had replaced the mattress and washed the bedding, but it still felt like her mother's bed. She threw back the covers and climbed in. The scent of her mother's perfume wafted gently to her nose as she got comfortable.

She was finally able to take in the beauty of the ornate box. Tracing the lid, she admired the details of the mother of pearl overlay.

The etched design was a floral theme and had leaves and flowers throughout the box. As she reached out to run her fingertip over the largest flower on the top of the lid, she quickly realized what it was supposed to be.

"Oh!" She exclaimed happily. "They're peonies. Of course. Of course they're peonies!" She laughed.

Running her hands over the lid of the box, she rested them a moment on each side. This was going to be an adventure, to see what memories were in the box. Taking a deep breath, she slowly opened the lid to reveal what was inside.

It was like a mini treasure chest.

The box was inlaid with a deep red velvet lining, and the scent of peonies wafted up from the contents. The container had a tray that held a variety of items; ticket stubs from movies and shows, a couple of old school subway tokens from the '90s, two random root beer bottle caps, several of the pressed pennies from around the city, and a small five-by-seven-inch sketchbook.

Immediately, she opened up the sketchbook. Inside, she recognized her mother's handwriting on the cover page. It read, 'The Wondrous Adventures of Gabby and Xan' in her sprawling script. Calli traced her mother's name before flipping through the little book. It was full of little stories about what adventures they had been on that day. According to the first entry, their first date was actually to The Argosy Bookstore. Her father had purchased this sketchbook for them there at her mother's insistence. Her mother had even used the receipt as a bookmark.

Besides the stories of her parents' various dates, there were also sketches of different moments of their time together. A sketch from their first breakfast in bed, various sketches of flowers and trees, a close-up drawing of her father's hands holding onto a coffee cup. All these little moments during their life together, captured through her mother's words and drawings.

Wedged in between the back pages of the sketchbook was the key to the lock on the box. The key was made of silver and had more of the mother of pearl inlay on the top part of the key, or the bow. As she continued looking it over, she realized the design on the bow was not just the same leaves as the box itself, but it was a miniature version of the peony on the box. It was beautiful.

"I wonder how it would look on a necklace," she said to herself. That would be something she would look into soon. But there was still so much to discover in the keepsake box.

Quickly sorting the items from the top tray, she pulled it from the box and set it to the side. Inside the box were a couple wine corks with dates written on their ends, more photos and drawings, various play-bills from the Broadway shows they went to, as well as a little stuffed moose that had two cheap novelty rings stuck on his antlers. There was also another small three-by-five-inch Moleskine notebook that smelled very strongly of peonies.

She quickly sorted all the playbills to the side so she could look at the photos and drawings in more detail. All the moments were captured in sketch or image. She could not decide which she liked better.

The photographs were amazing little snapshots into their time together. There were two that were her absolute favorite pictures. The first was the close-up image of them laughing while her father was holding her mother in his arms. The second was an image of the two of them holding hands while walking over the Brooklyn Bridge. Her mother was leading the way and her father had slowed to snap the photo the moment her mother looked back to see why he was walking so slowly. The look of joy and happiness on her face was amazing. Calli was so happy her father had captured this moment.

Using the larger of the two notebooks, she was able to piece together their time together. Her mother even had the foresight to put the dates on the backs of the drawings and images. That way, she could go back to the notebook of all their adventures together and read the corresponding story. Being able to go back and experience their life together just added to the magic of it all.

She picked up the little moose and looked closely at the rings. They were simple little plastic rings, one blue and one red, made into the shape of a heart. There was no date written on the moose, so she had to thumb through the sketchbook to find the entry corresponding to it.

April 10th, 1996

Today we went to Coney Island and had a picnic on the beach of chili dogs, cheese fries, and popcorn. Then we played games in the arcade. Xan won me the wonderful little moose, and I won us the two rings. I'm apparently a wiz at that skee-ball game. We made a promise to always wear the rings, especially when we aren't together.

We had a wonderful day today. Dancing in the middle of the crowd on the boardwalk was my favorite moment. Xan knows that whenever I want to dance, he has to oblige. He pretends to get grumpy about it, but I know he secretly enjoys it.

We ended the day by riding the Wonder Wheel, sharing several kisses underneath the stars and the bright lights of Coney Island. It truly was an exceptional day.

Calli leaned back against the pillows and smiled. Her mother had made sure to record every little moment with her father, and that allowed Calli to see past her father's gruff and business-like exterior. This was a wonderful gift.

"Thank you, Mom," she said to the box and traced the peonies on the lid again. "I will cherish it forever."

She woke up the next morning to Aretha calling her.

"Child! Where on earth are you?!"

Groaning loudly, she sat up. It took her a few moments to realize she was still in her mother's bed, the contents of the memory box spread out around her. "I'm in here, Aretha," she called.

Aretha entered and took in the scene. Calli was propped up on the bed surrounded by all the items from the mother of pearl box. The box itself was right next to her, the lid still propped open and the tray next to it. "What on earth is stuck to your face?"

"What?" Calli gasped and reached up with both hands to feel what was on her face. "Oh my gosh, what is it?" She panicked.

It was one of the bottle caps from the box. Apparently, she had fallen asleep on the mementos her mother had saved of their time together and the bottle cap had stuck to her cheek.

She quickly grabbed it and set it in the tray. "These are all memories of my mother and father's time together. I guess I fell asleep while I was going through it last night. I still haven't even touched some of it."

"Well, you'll have to finish going through this later. We have a date with the models today! And you need to finish the alterations. So, get up, girl! Let's get to it."

Today, Aretha was wearing a lime green tube top and neon pink dress pants. Her shoes matched the lime green from the top.

"Are those the Saint Laurent sandals? They are gorgeous!"

"They are. I was inspired by the stephanotis and tulip dresses your mom made so I decided to make a flower outfit of my own."

"I love it, I really do."

"Now, get out of that bed and the mess of things. We've got stuff and things to do! I've already got more pastries in the kitchen. Let's get some breakfast and get to it."

Calli's stomach rumbled in agreement. "Okay, breakfast it is. Then I have to go get the rest of those dresses altered. It shouldn't take me too long."

"Oh, and I had the outfit you wore last night laundered. Those pants of yours were such a huge hit with Kayla I figured you should wear them today. Although, we will have to see if your mom has any tops in her closet for you to wear. I like the top you made, but it is tragically boring. And we can't have you in boring outfits when you are meeting with the models."

"Any chance I have to go through my mom's closet is always a plus in my book."

"So, you go grab some breakfast, and I'll go see what I can find in your mom's closet. Deal?"

"Deal!" Calli quickly got out of the bed, careful not to disrupt anything, and ran into the kitchen to go get some of the pastries.

"These pastries are amazing!" she sang from the kitchen as she devoured a chocolate croissant. She went about making a black tea for herself and one for Aretha.

Carrying both of the teas, she walked back into her mother's room and made a beeline for the closet. "Here, I made you some black tea. What have you found?"

Aretha took the tea from her. "Thank you, dear. This is exactly what I needed." She had gathered a few tops. The first was a lilac-colored peasant-style top. It reminded Calli of the pink peasant dress Aretha had worn yesterday. The second was a black and white striped long sleeve top. The third was a high-necked sleeveless silk top that was off-white with a floral print.

"Hmmm... I like them all, but I have no idea which one I should wear."

"Well, here are the pants you made. Why don't you put them on and try on the tops to see which one you like best?"

"I thought you said you had sent them out to be laundered. How did they come back so fast?"

Aretha just smiled and handed them to her. "Magic, of course."

"Oh, of course. How silly of me." She quirked her brows at Aretha and took the hangers for the shirts she offered her. "I'll be right back."

She went into the bathroom to try the tops on. The purple peasant top fit her perfectly, but it was a little too casual for meeting the models. The flower print top fit her perfectly as well, but it was a bit too fancy for an informal meeting. The striped top was the best option, she decided, but she was not completely sold on it.

Walking back into the closet wearing the striped top, she asked, "Does this look okay? I'm not sure."

The top fit her perfectly, like it was made for her, but it was a little bit shorter than what she normally chose to wear. You could see a tiny bit of stomach because of the cut on the shirt.

"Darling, it looks great! What are you so nervous about?"

"I don't normally like showing any extra skin. Does that make sense? I'm so pale and—I don't know. I guess I'm not used to it...."

"Well, you look fabulous so I wouldn't worry about it! And those pants really are something wonderful. Maybe I'll have you make ME a pair when we are all done with the show."

"Oh, I'd love to do that. Consider it a thank you for all the help you've given me."

"You are welcome, dear. Now, let's finish up those dresses of your mother's."

Chapter 18

Calli spent the next hour working on the edits for the other flower dresses. They were almost completely done but just needed to be cleaned up. She searched through all the outfits to make sure there were no stray threads or unfinished stitches. It did not take her very long at all.

As she was finishing the last of the dresses, she kept staring at the sweet pea dress. She felt as thought there was something missing from all the dresses, but she was not sure what it was.

Aretha came over and stood next to her a moment before asking, "What's going on? You've been staring at this dress for the last ten minutes or so."

"It's missing something, but I don't know what. They all are." Calli frowned. She spun the dress on the mannequin hoping to jar whatever idea she had loose.

"Hmmm...I have no idea. They seriously look amazing now that you've finished them."

"Thank you. It's my mom's designs though. I just finalized everything."

"True, but they are beautiful regardless. Hmmm..." Aretha stood next to Calli as they looked over the piece, resting her thumbs in her pants pockets as she contemplated.

Calli glanced from Aretha to the dress. Then Aretha again. "Oh my god."

"What?" Aretha asked.

"Pockets. They need pockets!" Calli shouted excitedly.

Aretha laughed and took a step back. "Are we done shouting now?"

Calli blushed. "Yes, sorry, I just got a little excited. Pockets are key."

"Oh, I definitely agree. Will you be able to tell if the dresses have pockets? Or will they be a surprise?"

"I think it should be a surprise. Most dresses don't have pockets built in, but things are changing. Hopefully more designers will start putting in pockets in dresses. And not those silly little ones that will barely hold a lipstick. They need to be legit-sized pockets."

Calli went to the sweet pea dress and looked at it carefully. *Where can I add the pockets? It needs to make sense for the person wearing it, and also not be completely obvious...*

She carefully inspected the dress and found that where her mother had placed each of the five petals, there just so happened to be the perfect spot for a pocket to go. Eagerly, she checked the other dresses to see if they were similar. It either seemed like her mother knew she would want to add pockets, or perhaps was going to be adding some herself. All the dresses had an ideal spot to add a pocket.

"My mom is a genius. Seriously," she told Aretha as she turned the sweet pea dress so she could show her. "See how here on the sweet pea dress she placed all the panels just so—so there's room for a pocket? It's the same on all of the dresses she made. Even the two rose dresses have an area that is perfect for pockets. She was brilliant."

"Oh yes, she definitely was." Aretha smiled.

Calli was able to add the pockets to each of the dresses in record time with Aretha there to help. When she had completed the last of the dresses, she lined them all up in front of the floor-to-ceiling windows.

Calli spun each of the dresses slowly, one by one, watching to see if the pockets were obvious or not.

"Oh, that's brilliant. Will you be able to tell that they have pockets when the models are wearing them?" Aretha asked.

"No. I mean, I don't think so. We will see when we have the models try them on. I'm so excited to meet everyone."

Aretha nodded then gave Calli a scrutinizing look. "You need to go get ready for when the models get here. We can't have you looking like you were up all night. Now go."

While she was getting ready, Gary arrived and started helping Aretha clear the space in the workroom. Derrick had mentioned he gathered at least fifteen models, and although the apartment itself was an open floor plan, it would undoubtedly get a little crowded.

Aretha had arranged for two portable changing rooms, and they were set up on the far wall next to the bathroom. Calli was so thankful for Aretha. She could not imagine doing this without her.

Aretha and Gary had also moved the two giant tables from the center of the room to in front of the windows so the tables were out of the way. They had also arranged the dresses in two staggered lines in the center of the room.

Calli noticed the covers were back over all the dresses. As she walked in, she asked, "Why are all the dresses covered, Aretha?"

"Well, we want this show to be a surprise, don't we?" Aretha asked as she walked over to where Calli was standing.

"Yes, but I don't mind if the models see the dresses."

"You don't, but in the world of camera phones and Instagram, we need to make sure that no one takes any pictures or posts anything about the show beforehand. We want a buzz about the show, but we don't necessarily want to give away the farm, so to speak."

Calli chuckled. "No, you are right. I didn't even think about that."

"Exactly! That's why Gary and I had your lawyer, Kenneth, write up a nondisclosure agreement. No one that comes tonight will be able to talk about it, take pictures, or post on social media unless they have your written consent."

"That seems a little strict, but I obviously don't know anything about social media or whatever, so thank you. I want people to see my mother's designs but not until after the show, you know?"

"I do. Gary is in charge of handing them out and making sure all the models sign before we show them the dresses."

She smiled. Gary, of course, was the perfect person to get the signatures. Just one look at him and you could tell he meant business. He was wearing another one of his three-piece suits in a deep royal blue, with a crisp white button-up shirt and one of the most beautiful ties she had ever seen. It was the same blue of his suit but the rose-like design was etched in a bright teal color. Calli thought it was perfect.

"Gary, you look wonderful. Well, you alway look impeccable, but I love this color on you. That tie is amazing."

"Thank you. It's one of my favorite ties." He smiled at her and looked over her outfit choice. "I love this look. Are those the pants you made that Aretha has been telling everyone about?"

Calli chuckled. "Yes, these are the ones."

He made a motion for her to spin in front of him, so she obliged. "I've worn these before. I'm sure you've seen me in them."

"I have. But it's different now, knowing that YOU made them. They really are fantastic. Do you do men's clothing? I'd love to have a pair or two of your pants."

She blushed. "Really? Wow, okay! I'll be honest, I've never made any men's clothing, but I'm sure I can figure it out. I mean, pants are pants after all." She shrugged.

"Well, let me know whenever you want to get my measurements and whatever else you'll need from me."

"Oh, I definitely will. Thank you again, Gary."

Aretha was eavesdropping and came over when Gary went to go make himself a coffee. "He's really warmed up to you, hasn't he?"

"Who? Gary?"

"Yes." Aretha smiled. "He's not normally so friendly. I've actually never seen him act the way he does with you. Only around his children and grandchildren, honestly."

"Wait. He has kids? And he's married?"

"Oh, yes. He and his wife, Sheila, have been married for well over forty years. They have three children and seven grandchildren." Aretha smiled again. "I just blew your mind, right?"

"Oh yes, definitely! I hope I get to meet them all someday soon."

"I'm sure you will. He really likes you, as I've said."

"I like him a lot too." Calli smiled. She was honestly starting to regret having to go home. The thought reminded her that she still needed to call her aunt.

"Oh! Excuse me a moment, Aretha. I'm going to call my aunt really quickly before the models start showing up, okay?"

Aretha nodded.

Calli grabbed her cell phone from her purse and called her aunt. As the phone was ringing, she heard a knock at the door. She let the phone ring a few more times, but her aunt didn't pick up. Sighing, Calli hung up to go answer the door.

"Hey, Derrick!" Calli beamed when she saw who was knocking. "Thanks again for arranging everything for the model meet and greet. I can't imagine doing this all on my own."

"You are welcome. Has anyone arrived yet? I know I'm early, but I also know how eager everyone is to meet you and see your mom's designs," he said as they walked into the studio apartment.

"No, no one has shown up yet, which is fine. I'm trying not to get nervous. Twenty or so models is a lot of people."

"Um…it might be more than that. You see, they all told their friends who told their friends…. So I don't know exactly how many to expect, but I invited fifteen of the models I've worked with. And I think your dad invited some as well."

She looked up at Derrick, her eyes wide. "Really? That's a lot of people. And I know this apartment isn't tiny, but it's not huge either.… I hope we all fit!" She laughed nervously.

He reached over and took her hand in his giving it a squeeze. "You'll be great. I'm sure of it. And the models are all so excited to meet you."

"Thanks, Derrick." She squeezed his hand back. "I have a serious question though. Okay?"

"Um okay…" He looked at her quizzically.

"I do NOT look like the Hamburglar, right? 'Cause if I had the little hat and the mask, I feel like that's what I would look like."

He burst out laughing. An absolute full-belly roar. It took him a few moments to catch his breath when he was done. Gary and Aretha both looked over at them. She thought she saw Aretha shake her head, but they did not say anything.

"Oh man, that was good. I totally wasn't expecting that," Derrick said as he finally stood up straight.

"Thanks. I have my moments." She straightened his collar. "I look okay though, right?"

"Yes, you look beautiful." He tucked a stray curl behind her ear. "Absolutely nothing like the Hamburglar."

"Calli, dear. I think we've got our first model!" Aretha called out in a sing-song voice.

Calli turned to the front door as the most beautiful woman she had ever seen entered. She was tall, of course, but the way she carried herself made Calli instantly think she was possibly royalty. Her deep brown skin glowed with a natural warm undertone. As she took the clipboard Aretha offered her, she smiled, and her eyes danced with happiness. Her dark hair was swept up into a high bun at the top of her head. She was wearing a cute purple tank top and plain black jeans.

Calli waited for her to finish filling out the NDA before going over to introduce herself. "Hi! I'm Calli. Thank you so much for coming," she said, offering her hand.

"It's my pleasure! I'm Lydia Thomas. When Derrick mentioned we'd possibly be modeling some of Gabriella's work, I had to come. There's no way in the world I would miss this." She took Calli's hand in both of hers and squeezed gently.

"Nice to meet you, Lydia. We will wait until the other models arrive, but I can't wait to show you the dresses my mom made."

Lydia rubbed her hands together eagerly. "Ooh, I can't wait!" She did a little happy dance, the heels of her shoes making cheerful light stomping noises. Calli smiled when she recognized the pair of So Kate Louboutins that she was wearing.

"I have those exact same shoes," Calli said, smiling from ear to ear.

"Girl, these are my go-tos! Whenever I have a go-see or casting call, these bad boys and I are there."

Just then, five other models walked in. Aretha and Gary immediately started handing out the NDAs.

Calli smiled at Lydia and nodded to the new arrivals. "Please excuse me. Feel free to have a look around. I'll show all the dresses once I've decided on the models. At least, I think that's what we should do! I've never done one of these, so I have no idea." Calli laughed.

"So far, you are doing great! And you have Derrick here. This isn't his first go-see either I think, so he'll be able to help."

Calli looked over to Derrick who was currently handing one of the other models a clipboard. She smiled softly remembering their date. "I totally should've kissed him last night."

Lydia laughed.

"Shit. Did I say that out loud?" Calli asked, turning a deep red.

"Yes, yes you did. But it's okay. I won't tell him what you said. But you are going to have to tell me more later, okay?!"

Calli chuckled. "Of course I will."

Chapter 19

In total, twenty-eight models of all ages and ethnicities, came to the meet and greet. Calli could not believe the love they had for her mother and was amazed so many came.

They were all gathered around the dresses, talking in various groups, waiting patiently for Calli to decide who was going to wear each one.

Calli whispered to Aretha, "I don't know who to pick for which dress. Honestly, the models are all so beautiful."

Aretha whispered back, "Well, why don't we start with the sweet pea dress and see who looks best in it? And then we can try that for each one?"

Derrick overheard and cleared his throat as he stepped closer. "Why don't you let the models decide which dress they'd like to model? You can have them line up by each one of the dresses and then they can all take turns trying that dress on? Models hardly ever get to choose what they are going to wear in shows, and I think this will be a treat for them. I brought my camera, so if you have a hard time deciding right now, I'll take pictures of each one so you can look at your favorites again later."

"Oh, that's a really good idea, Derrick! Thank you!" Calli beamed at him.

Calli walked into the middle of the room and called outsaid, "Excuse me! Everyone!"

She waited a moment to make sure she had everyone's attention. "I just want to thank you all for coming. The fact that all of you came means so much to me. My mom would have been so happy and excited to see every single one of you."

She cleared her throat a moment before continuing. Bringing up her mom made her start to tear up a bit. "Obviously, I don't have enough dresses for you all, but I would absolutely love to show you all the dresses,

145

and then have you all line up behind your favorite dress. We will have you try them on before I pick who will wear what in the show. Okay?"

The models all nodded, some of them—including Lydia—clapped with glee.

"I'm going to uncover each one of the dresses now that you have all signed the nondisclosure agreement. Please keep in mind that no one has seen these besides Derrick, Gary, Aretha, and myself."

She went over to the first mannequin, took a deep breath, and uncovered it. She did not know why she was so nervous about showing them all the dresses, but she was practically shaking.

What if they all hate it?! What if they see them and start laughing? Oh, that would be absolutely devastating...

But she did not need to worry. They all took in a collective gasp as the white rose dress was revealed.

"Oh my god. It's beautiful!" One of the models exclaimed.

Calli quickly moved on to the next, uncovering the tulip-inspired dress. Another collective gasp escaped the crowd.

She could feel herself beaming, as she uncovered each dress one by one until the red rose dress was the only one left. "This one is our favorite," she said as she smiled at Gary.

There was an audible "wow" as it was revealed.

"Feel free to look at each of the dresses before deciding which one you want to try on! And if there's more than one that you want to try on that is okay too! We don't have a set ending time so as long as you guys want to stay, you can stay. But I do turn into a pumpkin at midnight." She laughed happily.

The models immediately went to the dress that they felt most drawn to. Some of the dresses had two or three models, whereas the two rose dresses drew the longest lines.

"I see you guys have picked the first dress you want to try on! That was pretty quick!" She smiled broadly at them all as she turned her head. "Hey, Derrick, come here for a second."

He reluctantly went up beside her in front of the crowd.

"Some of you may know Derrick. He's a fashion photographer and has been a huge help while getting this all organized. He will be taking photos of you all in each of the dresses just in case we have more than one model that the dress looks great on. I have a feeling that may happen with a couple of the dresses."

Derrick waved. and said "Hello, everyone."

Calli smiled again and motioned for Aretha and Gary to come up as well. "These two are Aretha and Gary."

Aretha did the sweetest little curtsy at the sound of her name, and Gary, of course, just nodded.

"Aretha was not only my mom's best friend, but she's quickly becoming mine as well. I seriously could not have done anything like this without her." She wrapped her arm around Aretha's waist giving her a sideways hug.

"Gary is a makeup and hair magician. He's incredibly talented, and I am blessed to be able to learn from him. Thank you, Gary."

She thought she saw Gary blush for a moment, but it must have been her imagination because he nodded to her again.

"Okay! It's time to try on the dresses. Please, please be careful with them! They are truly one of a kind."

Calli had thought that after seeing the models try on the dresses, she would instantly know which dress should be worn by which model. But sadly this was not the case.

"Okay, guys! Let's all gather round please," Calli called out to the models.

"Thank you all for coming out. The fittings went better than I expected, so I will be looking over the photos Derrick took tonight. I promise to call you tomorrow after five to let you know if you've been selected for the show. We are still ironing out all the details, but we should have a location and date very soon." The models all laughed at her unintentional pun.

"Please, please make sure you have all left your contact information so I can call you tomorrow." She clasped her hands and continued, "Thank you, again. I can't tell you all how much…" A few tears started running down her cheeks. "Sorry about that," she added as she wiped the tears from her eyes.

After taking a deep breath, she finally was able to say, "I can't tell you how much all of you coming tonight has meant to me. I will cherish this memory forever."

After her emotional speech, the models all came over to say goodbye and to thank her for allowing them to see her mother's dresses. She almost started crying again, but she was able to maintain her composure.

Lydia waited until she was the last model left before coming over to say goodbye. "My momma always says, 'It's best to be the first one to arrive and the last one to leave.'" She smiled warmly at Calli. "I am so thankful for this opportunity and being able to meet you! My home base is here in New York City so please don't hesitate to call me if you need anything! I can't sew, but I know all the best places to go when you want to get pampered. My masseuse is a complete goddess and will absolutely get you right."

She surprised Calli by giving her a cheerful hug. It took Calli only a moment before she returned it warmly.

"Thank you so much for coming. I'm sure I'll be seeing you again very soon," Calli said as they pulled apart.

"Definitely! You need to explain what you were talking about earlier." She wiggled her eyebrows and pointed her chin to Derrick. Thankfully, he was busy setting up his photo printer and missed Lydia's shenanigans.

"Shhhh...!" Calli laughed. "I promise I'll tell you everything after the show, okay?"

"Deal! I'll talk to you tomorrow. Have a great night." She waved as walked out the door.

Calli walked over to see how Derrick was doing with the printer. "Thank you for taking the pictures of the models tonight. And printing out the photos! This is pretty cool, actually."

"Yeah, this is my 'portable' one. I have another one at home that I print my large prints on. That baby is a stay at home model and is absolutely not portable." He chuckled. "I have a few more to print, but then I'm done. Do you want to bring these over to Aretha and Gary?" he asked as he handed her a stack of photos.

"Sure!" Calli smiled at him and took the photos.

Their fingers touched for a moment and he smiled warmly at her. "Do you have dinner plans?"

She blushed and tucked a stray hair behind her ear. "No, not yet. Did you want to go get an early dinner?" It was almost five o'clock, and she was starving.

"I know of a great Chinese food place. They have the best lemon chicken. And it's real homemade lemon chicken. Not any of that pre-made sauce crap."

"That sounds great. Let me give these to Aretha and Gary and then maybe we will go? I can't think about choosing which model works best for which dress on an empty stomach."

"Okay, I'll bring the last few photos over when they are done printing."

She grinned. "Okay. I'll meet you over there."

Aretha and Gary were busy sorting the nondisclosure agreements along with the headshots of each of the models at the two large tables set up in front of the wall of windows.

"I've got most of the images of the models in the dresses. I figured I'd sort them and add them to the little piles you guys have here," Calli said as she approached.

Aretha turned and gave her a menacing look. Gary just smirked at her. "What?! What did I say?"

"I overheard you two talking. You two are going to go get dinner. Gary and I will finish sorting the photos. Don't you worry."

Calli offered her the stack of photos in her hand. "Okay, then. Thank you—*both* of you."

Gary looked over at her and said, "You better get going. Once Aretha has her mind made up, there is no way of changing it." He shrugged. "Besides, it won't take us long to get these sorted. And I have a hot date with my wife."

Calli smiled, "I cannot wait to meet her. Please tell me you will be bringing her with you to the show?"

Gary looked stunned for the briefest moment, but quickly regathered his cool demeanor. "Oh yes, she will come. I didn't realize we were invited…."

"Of course you're invited! I could not have done any of this without you. You MUST come."

"We will definitely be there." Gary smiled. A genuinely deep smile that made Calli very happy.

"Great!" Calli beamed again.

Chapter 20

Dinner with Derrick was yet another wonderful adventure. Honestly any moment she could spend with him was a huge plus. The Chinese restaurant was a tiny place that had more outdoor seating than inside. She would have never picked it based on its appearance, but the lemon chicken was beyond amazing. Even better, this time, Derrick let her pay.

"We will take turns, okay?" he asked when the waitress brought the bill.

"Absolutely!" She liked that he had not mentioned that she was supposed to leave after the show and it seemed like they had no expiration date. *Maybe they do not need to have an expiration date. Maybe. Maybe she could stay?*

Of course she could not stay in New York. How was she going to keep an eye on her aunt if she was on the other side of the country?

She was once again reminded that she still needed to call her aunt. "Shit," she muttered as she gathered up her purse to look for her phone.

"What?"

"Oh, I forgot to call my aunt. Do you mind if I call her on our walk back to the apartment?"

"No, I don't mind. I know how close you two are, so please call her."

"Thank you."

Once they were outside and had started walking, she dialed her aunt. But she did not pick up.

"Hmm, that's strange. She didn't answer. And she always answers."

"Maybe she went out to dinner or a movie or something?" Derrick asked.

"Maybe, but that's not really her MO. She's definitely a homebody and hardly ever goes out," she said furrowing her brows. "This is the second time she hasn't answered."

"I'm sure she's fine. She's a tough lady." Derrick took her hand in his and gave it a squeeze as they walked.

"This is true." She squeezed his hand back.

They walked together, hand in hand, for a moment before Calli said, "I think I'm going to sort through the models' photos when we get back, if that's okay? I have a feeling it's going to take me a while before I know which dress should be worn by what model. I hope it doesn't take long."

"Honestly, who cares if it does? This is supposed to be a show honoring your mother and the dresses she left you. This is something important, not only to you, but everyone involved. I just know your mom is watching over everything going on and is so incredibly proud of you."

She blushed deeply. "You can't say stuff like that to me."

"Why not?"

"Because that will make me want to stay. I really don't want to go back to Oregon…"

"Then don't?" He stopped and tucked that same errant strand of hair behind her ears.

"I worry about my aunt though. I'm the only one she has left now." She bit her lip softly.

"I understand. The only reason I'm able to live here in New York and not in Massachusetts is because my sister literally lives right next door to my mom. So I always have a way of checking on her." He squeezed her hand and they started walking again.

"It's tough being away from family, but you can make it work. If you do decide to stay, you will just need to make sure you talk all the time. Not necessarily every single day, but at least a couple times a week. I go see my family at least a few times a year. I love all the seasons in Mass so it's easy to go back every season. Fall is my favorite."

"Fall is my favorite too." She squeezed his hand again.

They had finally reached her apartment building and were walking up to the entrance. Were they both walking incredibly slow to draw out the walk? Yes. Would they admit it to each other? Of course not.

"Don't worry about walking me up. I'm good." She turned so that she was standing in front of him and took both his hands in hers. "Thank you...for everything you've done. I feel like I will forever be telling you thank you." She smiled and kissed first one hand then the other.

"You have my cell number so please call me if you have any questions or anything. I'll pick up my printer tomorrow, okay?"

"Yes, of course! I forgot about your printer. Do you want to come get it now?"

"Nah. This will just give me a reason to come by tomorrow." He smiled and took his turn kissing both of her hands.

"I'll see you tomorrow."

"Goodnight, Calli."

"Goodnight, Derrick."

She spent the rest of the evening choosing the models. For most of the dresses, she instantly knew who needed to wear them.

The rose dresses, however, were proving to be the toughest to match to their models. She absolutely loved the white dress on Lydia, but there was something off about it on her. And sadly, that was the case for the other dresses in the collection. They all looked absolutely great on Lydia, but there was something missing. And it was driving Calli crazy because she could not put her finger on it. The red rose dress looked the best on her, but again something was missing.

Calli sighed and worked on separating the stacks into different piles—one for absolutely must wear this dress; one for this dress looks great on you but something's missing; and the sad no pile. It broke her heart that there were not enough dresses for everyone that came.

"I'll have to sleep on it. At least most of the dresses have their match." She said aloud to herself as she placed the last couple of photos in their correct piles.

She quickly turned off the lights in the studio and went into the kitchen to make herself a cup of tea. When it was ready, she grabbed the box that held The Shoes from the coffee table and took them into her mother's room.

After setting the shoe box on the bed, she changed into the sushi pajamas and got into bed. She was careful not to dislodge any of the items sorted around her. Once she was settled, she opened the silver box and carefully took The Shoes out of their respective dust bags. She propped them up against the box, making sure that she would be able to see the stars on the bottoms.

Calli looked at everything spread around the bed and smiled. She loved how her mother had made a point to record every moment she and her father had spent together. *I will have to get a notebook like Mom used for her and Dad's adventures. For me and Derrick. If I stay...*

It was not late in the evening, but Calli was wiped. She decided it was better to go to sleep than to continue going through the items in the keepsake box.

She grabbed the box to start putting everything back in when she noticed there was a little velvet tab in one of the corners at the bottom of the box. She flicked it and realized it seemed to be attached to the bottom of the box. "That's weird."

Calli reached and pulled the little tab gently. With very little pressure it opened up to reveal a little space underneath it.

"Mom. We need to have a little talk about you hiding stuff away. Why on earth would you hide this?"

It turned out to be yet another hardbound sketchbook, but instead of regaling the time spent with her father, it laid out her mother's process of making all of the different flower dresses. As she thumbed through the journal, she was shocked to find not only information detailing the fabrics and accessories used, but also drawings of all the dresses. From her initial thought to a colorful final drawing of each dress.

"Oh, oh this would have been so helpful to find when I had first started altering them!"

As she flipped through the sketchbook she came to sketches of what she assumed would be the final dress of the collection. "She was actually making a peony dress!" Calli clapped with glee.

She eagerly flipped through all of the images of the peony dress until she got to the final sketch. And wedged between the pages was another note from her mom.

My Dearest Calliope,

I see you have found my secret sketchbook. I am so happy that your father gave you this box of all our memories in it. I hope you have started to see what a wonderful man he truly is and have enjoyed reading and seeing all the adventures we went on.

As you can see by now, I never did have time to start or complete the peony dress. I will always regret this fact and I am so sorry you will never be able to see it. It truly would have been astoundingly beautiful.

I'm sorry I failed you by not completing this dress. I know how much you adore peonies. They are our favorite flower after all.

I hope these sketches and drawings do bring you some kind of peace and hopefully you will forgive me.

- *Momma*

Calli wiped the tears streaming down her face. She hated that her mom felt like she had failed her. It absolutely broke her heart.

"I absolutely forgive you, Mom. Please don't ever think I'm mad at you. I just miss you oh so terribly." She had picked up her favorite photograph of her mother and father together. *I definitely need to get this framed. I bet Derrick or Dad knows of all the great places to go here.*

Flipping through all the sketches of the peony dress, she kept going back to the final drawing of the dress. Looking over her mother's design of the peony dress she had a crazy thought. *Maybe I can do this dress by myself. Mom left pretty clear instructions...and I know what I'm doing, at least in theory.*

Calli tapped her finger on her lower lip. "Hmmm..." Could she do it? The part that would be the toughest and take the longest to finish would be the top. She had only done a few corsets in her life, and it definitely was not something she wanted to do incorrectly.

What's the worst case? I make the dress and if it's awful, I don't show it? And this dress could be everything based on the drawing. It was that beautiful.

"I'll need to go see what I have in the workroom. I don't even know if I have any fabr..." she let the thought trail off as she remembered the red organza for Tony's shop.

Oh my god. That will be absolutely perfect for this dress!

Calli quickly gathered up the photos and mementos, and returned them to the box carefully. She made a point to leave the sketchbook, the beautiful key, and the picture of her parents out on top of the little chest and placed it on the nightstand.

Taking the sketchbook of the flower dresses, she ran into the workspace barefoot. When she was inspired, there was no time like now, right?

Chapter 21

Calli went to the two work tables and quickly set up the sketchbook by propping it open against the window. Grabbing the mood board her mother had made from on top of the bookshelves, she set that up next to the sketchbook.

She had originally thought of doing the toile, or the early version of the completed garment in the traditional muslin fabric, but she was afraid the fabric would not hang quite right, so she decided to look through what other fabrics she had on hand and try to match one to the organza.

As she was going through the different options, she kept going back to the red organza. "There's plenty of that fabric... if I mess it up, I can just start again. I have seventy-five or so inches. That should be more than enough." She said as she grabbed the organza and brought it over to the work table.

First she worked on the pattern for the dress. Her mother had, thankfully, detailed the measurements for each panel of the pattern for the core of the dress. The fun part would be adding the petals for the peony flower later. But she needed to make sure that the base of the dress was perfect.

As she was working on cutting out the pattern with the manila pattern paper, she kept thinking how beautiful this dress would look on Lydia. The red of the dress would just pop so beautifully with Lydia's complexion. So she changed the pattern to match Lydia's measurements exactly.

Hoping Lydia would be on board with her idea, she quickly finished the pattern and started cutting the individual pieces of the red silk. This part was absolutely nerve wracking. Yes she technically had extra

fabric, but she could not afford to mess up very much. She was confident in her sewing abilities, but an avant-garde dress was a whole other
world. She had only done a few avant-garde dresses herself. "If Mom
can do it, well then so can I!" she said to herself, bound and determined
to make it work.

Calli spent the rest of the evening getting the base of the dress completed. Tomorrow, she would work on the corset and possibly start on
the peony flowers. That would be the most exciting part of the dress.

She had decided she would only work on the dress at night when
she was completely alone. During the day, she would move it into her
old bedroom and keep it out of sight. She was sure that the dress would
be beautiful when it was finished, but she wanted to keep it a secret
until the night of the show.

"Super secret." She said to herself as she wheeled the mannequin
into the bedroom.

"It's like Mom had planned this all from the very beginning." She
smiled as she walked back into the workroom and gathered up the
sketchbook of the flower dresses.

She hugged it tightly to her chest as she headed back into her
mother's room.

Climbing into bed, she got comfy under the covers before opening
the sketchbook and looking at each of the flower dresses. Her mother
had put so much thought into each of the designs. Calli could only
hope that her mother would be proud as the models wore them down
the runway. Especially the two rose dresses and the peony dress.

As she was flipping through the sketchbook for the millionth time,
her doorbell rang. "What the heck! Who could that be?" Calli quickly
got up off the bed, the sketchbook falling and landing face down on
the floor.

"Dang it!" She had started to bend over to pick it up when the
person at the door started hammering on the door.

"Oh crap!" Calli threw her hands up in the air, then ran toward the
front door. It was only ten o'clock but that was still not an ok time to
be banging on someone's door.

"This had better be Aretha or Gary or someone is going to be in a world of hurt." She muttered to herself as she made sure the sushi pajamas and her hair were somewhat presentable.

She opened the door somewhat forcefully, then immediately gasped.

"What—what are you doing here?! Oh my god, come here!" The person standing at her door was the absolute LAST person she was expecting. It was her Aunt Maggie.

"Jeez! Took you long enough to answer the door. I was about to start kicking. I have been on a flight for forever and I'm tired."

"I'm so sorry, I was in bed. Come here!" Calli started crying the minute her aunt had completely enveloped her in her arms.

"No, absolutely not, dear! Don't you dare cry or I'm going to start crying too!"

"I am so happy you are here!" They finally stopped hugging after about two minutes and separated. "Wait. Why are you here?!" Calli asked.

Someone behind Maggie cleared their throat.

She looked up to realize it was her dad. "I'm so confused. What's going on?"

"Your father arranged to have me come! He even hired some professional people to come run the shop for us while I'm here! I told them not to touch a damn thing on my tables. They had better listen." She shot Xander a withering look.

Of course her aunt was most worried about keeping her crazy workspace the way it was.

"He came and picked me up from the airport too! I almost didn't recognize him, I mean it's been a million years since I've seen him last. The only reason I knew it was him was because he was holding a sign with my name on it. He didn't have balloons tho..." She sounded a little disappointed that she had not gotten the same welcome as Calli had, but she seemed happy.

"I am so excited for you to be here. Please come in, both of you!"

Her father shook his head, "Oh no. You guys go in and catch up. I'm going to get going, but I'll see you tomorrow? Maybe I can come over and we can all have dinner together?"

"Oh yes, that would be wonderful, Dad. Thank you so very much for arranging everything so Aunt Maggie could be here. I can't believe it!"

"The people I hired to help out at the shop own a few flower shops in surrounding cities. And the owner owed me a favor as I photographed his daughter's wedding, so Morgan's Flowers is in the best of hands. Don't you worry!" He smiled and gave them both a quick hug. "I'll see you guys tomorrow night, okay?"

"Okay! Thanks again, Dad." She smiled, her arm firmly wrapped around her aunt's waist. She still could not quite believe she was here. "Here, let me take that!" she said as she took the handle of her aunt's luggage.

As they walked into the apartment together, wheeling the luggage behind them, Calli took in what her aunt was wearing. A very brightly colored yellow vest that had different variations of bright pink flowers woven into the fabric. She had on a bright green long sleeve, button-up shirt, and her pants would undoubtedly make Aretha jealous as they were the same bright pink of the flowers on her vest.

"Aunt Maggie! I love your outfit! Is it new?" Calli asked as they stopped in the kitchen.

"Yes it is! I couldn't come to New York City and not dress more fashionable. I found this vest at the thrift store next door and I knew I needed to have it. It was only a dollar!" Her aunt puffed out her chest and then did a little spin to show it all off.

"I love it. I really do!" She was so happy that her aunt had come. Her not answering her phone was because she was on the plane coming here.

"I'm so ridiculously happy you are here, Aunt Maggie. Oh my gosh!" She immediately enveloped her in another hug. "I've really missed you."

"I've missed you too, dear." Aunt Maggie hugged her back.

"So what is going on here? The apartment is a little messy…not your normal operating style at all."

Calli laughed. "I know! It's weird, right? Normally I have everything so organized but I haven't had time! I've been too busy getting the show ready."

"Oh yes, you said you had found some dresses your mother had made. Can I see them?"

"Yes, please! They are all flower-themed dresses and I'm so inspired by them all. They are absolutely beautiful. Here! Let me show them to you."

Calli led her aunt over to where all the dress forms stood uncovered. "I'll let you take them all in."

"Okay!" Her aunt exclaimed gleefully as Calli watched her go to the first dress.

"Okay, I'll get started on the eggy toast while you get changed."

"Okay!" Aunt Maggie said, then she stopped mid-step. "I have no idea what to wear. You are having all the models come over later, right?"

"Oh, it doesn't matter. Wear whatever you want. Honestly. No one is going to judge. All the models are really nice. Also, feel free to look at all the clothes Mom has. I'm sure you can find something in there if you don't like what you brought."

"Alrighty then. I'll see what I brought with me and then I'll look through the closet to see if I like anything." She put her foot down and continued walking into the master bedroom. They had moved her suitcase into the closet, and Calli cleared enough space so her aunt could hang up anything she wanted.

After her aunt had wandered into the closet, Calli got started on making the French toast. She had just pulled the bread from the breadbox when the doorbell rang. She had a feeling it was going to be Aretha, but who honestly knew anymore?

She opened the door with a smile. "Good morning."

"Oh, good morning, dear! It's good to see you up and not dressed in your pajamas," Aretha huffed mockingly at her.

Today, she had raided her mothers closet and decided to wear the peasant top Aretha had found, and she had luckily found a pair of the traditional Levi's that fit without any help from Aretha. The jeans were happily the dark wash that she preferred. She had opted for the lower-healed Ferragamo Vara pumps today.

"Hey now. You bought me those pajamas, so they can't be all that bad."

"True," she agreed as she walked into the apartment. "So, what is on the agenda today?"

Her outfit today was a fitted pair of pale pink dress pants and matching pink button up that had black streaks in a random geometric design. Her hair was in a high bun on top of her head.

"So, I have some news," Calli announced as they entered the kitchen. "My aunt is here from Oregon. Dad apparently arranged the whole thing and dropped her off last night. I'm so excited she is here."

"That's wonderful, dear! I can't wait to meet her. I mean, we met when she came to gather you and your things after your mom died, but that was so many years ago."

"Did you want any French toast? I was going to make Aunt Maggie and I some before we went back to work in the studio. I've almost got all the models picked out. I just need help with the rose dresses. There are just too many good options to pick from!"

Just then, her aunt came in from the bedroom. "What do you think?" She did a slow turn to show off the outfit she picked out. The long sleeve top was a soft pink, but it was entirely made out of those tiny ostrich feathers. It almost completely enveloped her aunt's small frame. The long skirt was the same shade of pink, but had silver metal pieces stamped throughout the entire skirt, making up different shapes. And, of course, she was wearing a pair of Gabriella's heels.

She had picked out the same style shoes Aretha had been wearing the day she picked her up from the airport. The pink of the crystals sparkled as Maggie turned.

Aretha watched and then asked, "Are those the Louboutin Daffodile pumps? What a perfect choice! I especially love your pink top! I think I have a very similar one."

Calli had been slightly nervous about what Aretha was going to say about her aunt's outfit, but she should have known Aretha would make her aunt feel wonderful and welcome.

"Oh, I have no idea about the name of these, but I saw them and thought they would look great with my outfit. I want to look good for the models, you know?"

"I definitely do! Now, come sit with me while Calli makes us some breakfast. I've heard wonderful things about her French toast," Aretha said as she sat on the couch.

"Oh, yes. Calli makes the best eggy toast ever." Aunt Maggie smiled and sat next to Aretha on the couch.

Calli just smiled watching the two of them as they caught up. It was great seeing her aunt having fun.

The model fitting was an absolute blast. Calli had finally decided who was going to wear what dress, and called all the models over to do a final fitting. She wanted to make sure the dresses all fit perfectly.

Aunt Maggie was a hit with all the models. They absolutely adored her outfit. The compliments she kept getting made her night. Calli could tell by the way she was beaming.

She invited Lydia, of course, under the pretenses of being a backup in case one of the other models could not attend the event. But she pulled her aside and told her about the peony dress.

"It's not finished yet, I still have probably two days or so left, but it will be done by the time the show starts. I can show you the sketches and drawings my mom made. But this has to be hush hush. Super secret, okay?" Calli whispered.

"Ooh girl, how did you know I love super-secret secrets. I am definitely down. This is so exciting!" Lydia whispered back, a huge smile spreading across her face.

"I also have another idea, but it's still percolating in my head, but I may need your help with another super fun secret thing. If you are interested?"

"Absolutely! Oh, I'm so excited! I can't wait to hear more. You will tell me more as soon as possible, right?"

"For sure! Here, let me give you my cell phone number."

They exchanged numbers, and Calli had promised to call her when the peony dress was ready to be fitted.

As everything was wrapping up, Aretha came in and said, "Excuse me, ladies! Ladies! I have a VERY important announcement! Gather 'round, chickadees!"

Aretha waited until all the models were gathered around her. Calli stood toward the back with Lydia.

"Where's Calli?" Aretha asked, looking around the room. "Get up here!"

Calli made her way through the crowd of models before finally reaching Aretha. She stood next to Aretha awkwardly, not knowing what her announcement was.

"As you all know, I've been working behind the scenes trying to find somewhere to host this fashion show for Gabriella. I knew it would need to be someplace very special because, let's be honest, she was a very special lady." She smiled at Calli.

"So, I'm very proud to announce that..." Her smile grew even wider as Calli groaned softly.

"Sheesh, Aretha! Stop lollygagging and tell us all already!" Maggie cried, stomping the Louboutins in protest.

Aretha laughed. "We are going to be hosting it this weekend at The Great Hill in Central Park!"

The models all gasped and some of them, including Lydia, cheered.

"I've already been in contact with a company that will help us set up the tent, the runway, and all the lights and electrical needed. Gary, whom you all met at the casting, will be in charge of hair and makeup. I will oversee everything to make sure it all goes off without a hitch."

Calli was absolutely speechless for a moment.

She waited until all the models were done celebrating with Aretha before she pulled her aside. "I can't believe you were able to pull this off. Central Park? Really? How freaking amazing is this?"

"I know Belvedere Castle is a special place for you and your mom, but I just didn't have time to get the permits, security, and all that, to host a show there. I'm sorry."

"Please don't apologize! I was thinking we'd have to hold it in some hotel somewhere. Not in freaking Central Park! It doesn't matter if it's not at the Belvedere! The Great Hill will be absolutely perfect." Calli smiled brightly at Aretha. "I'm going to hug you now."

"Oh, sweet child, you never need to let me know you are going to hug me. Come here!"

Aretha enveloped her in a hug that made her feel absolutely safe. "Thank you again, Aretha."

"You are most welcome, dear."

Chapter 23

The next few days passed in a whirlwind of sewing, sewing even more, and trying to organize the show. Calli was so thankful for everyone in her corner and had no idea how to pay them all back, but she would definitely try.

Aretha was instrumental in organizing everything. She not only was able to get all of the permits needed for the show in record time, probably because she had the inside Fairy God Mother connection, but she was able to hire all the background staff that would be needed. And man, there was a ton of background people to hire.

Gary and Calli talked about the direction the hair and makeup would take. Calli had been inspired by the minimal makeup Gary had taught her when she had first arrived, so they decided to do a natural makeup look.

"The dresses are so beautiful, there's no reason to overload the models with a ton of makeup and crazy hair. I think a natural look with a pulled back romantic- styled hair will look best."

He had brought his portfolio to show her what he was talking about. Some of the looks matched exactly what they were both envisioning, and being able to see some of Gary's work in print was an amazing experience.

"You are so talented. Seriously," she murmured as she flipped through his portfolio.

"Thank you." He nodded, and she thought she caught the faintest smile.

In secret, Calli had almost completed the peony dress. It was turning out breathtaking. She just needed to finish a few more of the petals.

The corset took the longest time, since Calli was nowhere near being an expert. But with her aunt's encouragement, she was finally able to pull it off.

Aunt Maggie had become a major part in helping organize all of the dresses and their corresponding shoes. Calli had decided to go with basic black heels for all the models. She wished she was able to locate her favorite Benedettos, but unfortunately that would be impossible. The shoes were in such high demand they were either incredibly out of her price range or they would not arrive in time.

They only had one and a half days to make sure everything was all set and ready to go. Calli was starting to get very nervous, but she tried very hard not to let it show.

Derrick could see right through her facade, but he thankfully kept it to himself and was there to help in any capacity. From making sure she had food to eat and plenty of tea to drink, he also helped arrange for the various photographers that would be shooting the event.

Last, but not least, was her father. He allowed her and Aretha to have full access to all of his contacts—, and man did he have contacts. Aretha confessed that most of the people she had hired for the show were all referred by her father. He knew people in every facet of hosting a fashion show and had been an incredible help.

Calli took a moment to look around her at all the people helping and tears welled up in her eyes.

"Hey now. Don't you start blubbering like that. We can't have you breaking down in front of the crowd," Aretha said as she came up next to her.

"I know, I know, but I'm just so thankful for everyone. I know I keep saying this over and over again, but it's true. I could have never done any of this without each one of your help."

"I know, dear. But pulling off this show in less than a week is an amazing feat. You can thank us all after the show, okay?"

"Okay." Calli smiled. "Hey, Aretha, you pretty much know which purses my mom has in her closet, right?"

"Yes, of course I do."

"Well, are there any that would be big enough for me to carry all the little extras I might need for the show? You know, extra sewing supplies and the like?"

Aretha thought about that for a moment. "Hmm…your mom has a couple of the largest Hermès Birkin bags in there. One of those should probably work."

"Okay, awesome! I know nothing about purses or accessories really, so I thought I would ask the only pro I know." She giggled at the little rhyme.

Aretha just shook her head.

It was officially the night before the show. Everything was as ready as it was going to be. Calli had asked everyone to the studio apartment for dinner. Thankfully, her dad took charge and had arranged for the restaurant they had had their ill-fated dinner at, Lucca, to cater the event.

She was not sure how her father had been able to book such a last minute request, but she was incredibly happy. And of course the food was delicious.

Calli and her aunt were sitting after dinner going over the last-minute edits Calli had made to the peony dress. She had needed to move some of the panels of peonies to make sure the pockets fit in with the design like the other dresses.

Calli sketched the dress quickly on a napkin and showed her aunt where she thought she should place the pockets. "I can't believe I almost forgot the freaking pockets! Thank you so much for reminding me, Aunt Maggie."

"Oh of course, dear! I wouldn't let you show that piece without it being completely done. I noticed when the models were trying them all on the other day that they had pockets. This one should have them too."

"The food tonight was amazing wasn't it?" Calli asked as she watched her dad. He was telling one of the adventures he and Roland had gotten into, and the models surrounding him were hooked on his every word.

"Absolutely! It was delish." Her aunt patted her very full belly in appreciation.

"I'm so happy he finally came around and I was able to see the real him and not just this facade he puts on." She smiled; he had said something apparently very funny and all the models were laughing hysterically.

"What do you mean, 'finally came around'?"

Calli turned and looked at her aunt seriously. "Wait, what?"

Her aunt blushed. "Crap. Just ignore what I said."

"No, absolutely not! What are you talking about?"

"I don't want to tell you though! He should be the one to tell you!"

"Tell me what, Aunt Maggie?" She furrowed her brows at her aunt.

"Dang it. Don't do that with your eyebrows. Now I know you won't let this go. Dang it. I should have just kept my mouth shut. Shit."

Calli waited somewhat patiently for her aunt to finally tell her what she meant.

"He's always been in your life, Calli, but he's just stuck to the background. He didn't want you to know he has been keeping an eye on you because your mother wished it that way."

"What do you mean?" Calli asked, looking between her aunt and her father.

"Any big thing that happened to you, be it graduating from high school or college. He was there. I just didn't tell you about him being there because he didn't want to mess with your memory of your mom."

Calli stared at her father for a moment, completely shocked.

"He even went to your first ever play back in kindergarten. I think you actually were a flower."

Calli only vaguely remembered being in a play when she was that young. She had been one of many sunflowers.

"He also paid for all of your schooling. I know you thought you had gotten scholarships—and you did!—but, unfortunately, they didn't cover all of your tuition and living expenses. He took care of what the scholarships didn't."

"He did that?"

"Yes, yes he did. He really is an amazing man."

Calli immediately got up and went over to her father. The tale of his adventures with Roland had ended so the models had just dispersed.

"Oh, hey, Calli! I was just telling the models a story, did you want to—" He stopped mid sentence because Calli threw her arms around him and hugged him.

It took him a moment for the shock to wear off, but when it did, he enveloped her back.

"Thank you, Dad."

"For what?"

my lists a million times." She furrowed her brows going through her mental list a moment before shrugging and asking, "Do you want breakfast? I make a mean French toast."

Derrick laughed and shook his head. "I was thinking I could make you an omelette. I'm not too shabby around the kitchen myself."

"Okies, that sounds wonderful. And I need to refill my coffee."

"Oh! If I knew you wanted coffee, I would've brought you something from my favorite coffee place."

"I honestly don't drink it that often, so it's okay. I really only like the dark stuff that most people don't like. I hate the acidity in the lighter roasts, that's one of the reasons I don't really drink it. I'm kind of a coffee snob." She laughed again.

"Ah, okay. Well, we will have to go there and find one you really like then." Again they were avoiding talking about what would happen after the show and her going home.

"Oh, definitely. It's a date."

She and Derrick walked back into the main apartment. She showed Derrick where all the different ingredients were.

"So, the important question is, do you want a dessert-type omelette or a savory one? You've got your pick of ingredients here."

"Oh, a berry omelette sounds amazing. I figure I'll need the extra sugar to get through the day today." She laughed and went to make herself a refill of the coffee. "I'll make you a coffee if you want one?"

"Sure, I'll take whatever you are having." He got to work gathering all the ingredients to make the omelette.

After making the coffee, she sat down at the island and watched him make the omelettes. He reminded her of her dad a little bit, in all honesty, watching him move around the kitchen. Even though he did not know where everything was, he found it quickly and moved around the kitchen with such confidence. It was great just sitting there watching him work.

After a while, her aunt wandered in from the bedroom. "Hi, Derrick. Sorry I'm not dressed, but I wasn't expecting anyone to be here." She chuckled and pulled at her oversized sleep shirt.

Derrick laughed and said, "Oh it's quite all right. I've seen your niece in a similar outfit. Remember your New York shirt?"

Calli blushed. "Oh, I'd still be wearing it if I hadn't gotten these sushi pajamas. Trust me." She mockingly huffed at him, crossing her arms across her chest.

Derrick laughed then asked Aunt Maggie, "Would you like an omelette? I just finished this one for Calli. It's got all kinds of berries in it." He showed off the omelette he had made before placing it and a fork in front of Calli.

"Oh, yes please, it smells delicious. That's why I woke up, I think." She plopped down on one of the other chairs at the island, then turned to Calli. "So, today is the day then, isn't it?"

"Yes it is. I actually feel pretty confident. Everything is ready to go. As long as all the models show up, we should be good."

"That's good. You definitely want to be thorough. Are you nervous?" her aunt asked, studying her face.

"I'd be crazy not to be. I mean, this is my mom's legacy after all. How could I not be nervous?" She took a bite out of Derrick's omelette. "This is amazing, Derrick. Thank you!"

"You are welcome. I'll have yours up here in a second, Maggie."

"Thank you, Derrick." She looked back and forth between them and shook her head.

"What? Aunt Maggie?" Calli was almost afraid to ask.

"I can't believe you two have not kissed yet. What's up with that?"

Calli almost choked on her bite of omelette.

Derrick looked between the two of them with a sly smile. "Well, she's been distracted with getting ready for the show. It's okay. We have plenty of time." He made a point to hold Calli's gaze before turning back to cooking.

Calli flushed, and quickly finished the omelette. "Um, I'm gonna go get ready. Aretha and Gary will be here at six to help get everything loaded up into the moving van. I can't believe it's actually here." She brought the plate and fork to the sink and set them down. "Thank you for making us breakfast, Derrick." She stood up on her tiptoes to kiss him on the cheek.

"You are welcome." He smiled and leaned into her for a moment before turning back to the stove.

Aretha and Gary both showed up a few minutes before six and immediately took charge. Aretha had hired a company to move all of the dresses and items needed to the location in Central Park. And Gary overlooked everything.

Calli literally blinked and all of the items needed—the twelve huge boxes that held the dresses, the totes with the shoes and other extras, and everything else—were gone in a matter of minutes.

Calli walked up to Aretha and said, "If I ever move, I'm hiring you to manage all the details, because this all went off without a hitch."

Aretha smiled nonchalantly and flicked an imaginary piece of fluff off her arm. "Being a Fairy God Mother does have its perks."

Out of all the outfits Aretha had worn during her time in New York, Calli decided this outfit was hands down her favorite. It was a stunning sleeveless, full-length gown in a bright pink leopard print. Her blonde hair was in big beautiful curls that framed her face. Her makeup was flawless—a deep smokey eye that made her brown eyes pop.

"You look absolutely stunning. I love this dress!"

"Thank you, darling." Aretha curtseyed.

Calli was standing next to Aretha with her hands behind her back. "Let's get Gary over here for a moment? I have something for the two of you."

"Gary! Get your booty over here! Calli has something to give us!" she called.

Gary looked up and excused himself from the conversation he was having with the driver of the moving truck. He was wearing another three-piece suit, but completely black. His black tie matched the fabric exactly. The crisp white shirt underneath looked like it would repel any speck of dirt or anything that would mar its perfection.

"Gary, you look wonderful." She smiled at the two of them and then revealed both hands. She was holding two plain white boxes.

"I hope you don't mind, but I made you two something. It's just something small to say thank you for everything you have done. I literally CANNOT imagine being able to pull this all off without the two of you. I can't thank you enough." Calli held one of the boxes out to each of them. "I hope you like them." She thought she had been nervous enough about the show, but having them open their gifts made her anxiety shoot up.

Aretha squealed happily and immediately tore into the box. When she finally was able to see what was inside, she gasped. "Oh...Oh, Calli. It's beautiful! Will you help me put it in my hair?"

Calli obliged and helped Aretha attach the barrette to her hair. Of course, she had to bend over quite a bit so Calli could reach, but they managed. Aretha finally stood up and immediately went to the full-length mirror they had placed next to the changing rooms. "It's perfect! Truly! I absolutely love it and will cherish it forever."

It was a beautiful bright pink peony made from some of the silk she had left over from one of the dresses her mother had made. It matched the pink of her leopard dress perfectly.

"What do you think, Gary?" Calli had noticed he had opened his box quietly while she was assisting Aretha, but he was just standing there staring at the box.

"Calli. I…" He looked up, tears in his eyes. "I don't know what to say."

His gifts were a little red rose boutonniere made from the same material as the red rose dress, and a matching red tie. He touched one of the petals carefully, his hand shaking. "They are stunning."

"Do you want me to help you put them on? I was hoping you'd wear them to the show today."

"Yes, please." She could see how badly his hands were shaking when she took the box and just smiled. He removed his plain black tie and put the red one on. Calli had to help him get it in the correct place.

As she put the little red rose on his jacket, she caught a single tear fall from his eye. Wordlessly, she offered him a tissue. "There. It's all set."

He wiped the tear from his eye and quickly balled up the tissue and stuck it in his suit jacket pocket. He quickly walked over to the mirror and took in his reflection. He turned and took Calli's hands in his, "I love it, Calli, I really do. Thank you."

"You're welcome, Gary. It was absolutely my pleasure. After all your help, it was the least I could do."

Chapter 25

Backstage was practically a zoo. Calli had never seen so many people packed into such a small space. Not only were all twelve of the models there, but Calli had asked some of the models they were not able to use to come help. Thankfully, they were all very excited and willing to help with Gabriella's show.

Besides all the extra models now running around, there were also the professional dressers Aretha had hired to help get the models ready to walk the runway. They were not only able to help the models don the outfits, but they also were able to do any slight alterations that may come up at the last second.

"This is some kind of madness! Definitely a lifetime event. I'm so happy to be here!" Lydia said the moment she saw Calli who was currently helping the model into the red rose dress. "These all look beautiful," Lydia said as she gestured around her. "I cannot wait until later!" She touched her nose twice as she said the word later.

"I am so happy you came, Lydia. I cannot wait for later either!" Calli touched her nose twice and winked at Lydia.

"Kinda like a secret handshake!" Lydia had exclaimed when they came up with their signal.

Turning back to zipping up the dress, Calli smiled when she saw the little silver star at the top of the zipper line. Calli had decided late last night to go back and add the little star buttons Tony had given her to each of the dresses. And she had saved the sparkly one for the peony dress.

"Calli! Oh there you are!" Calli heard her aunt cry from behind her. Turning, she saw a flash of bright green and red before she was enveloped in a hug.

"Aunt Maggie! There you are. Did you get here okay? Sorry I left so early."

Her aunt pulled back from their hug and smacked her lightly on the arm. "Oh, pish posh. I got here just fine. Your dad was a perfect gentleman, as always, and came to pick me up."

"You look amazing, Aunt Maggie! Here, let me look at you."

Her aunt was wearing a bright green silk suit with thousands of tiny beads sewn in the shape of monstera leaves. She had even popped the collar on her bright pink shirt. Her normally wild red hair was slightly tamer than usual. Calli could tell that Gary had tried to help her with it, but her aunt being the stubborn person she is, most likely rejected his offer. The most exciting part was the fact that her aunt was absolutely beaming.

"I'm going to go find my seat before all the people start arriving. I don't want to get trampled by all the people I saw waiting to come in when I arrived. There was quite a crowd of people out there, so I think that's exciting."

"Oh, I think so too. I'm so happy you came." She hugged her aunt again before sending her off to find her seat.

"Aretha helped pick out her outfit, and Gary helped with the rest," Xander said as he walked up. Her aunt had run away from her father when she had caught sight of Calli. "She's a quick one when she wants to be." He chuckled. He was wearing a dark grey suit with black dress shoes.

"Hey, Dad. I'm so happy you came!" She went over and gave him a hug. "Can you wait here for a second? I have something for you."

"Okay."

She came back a moment later with another little white box. She handed it to her father and said, "It's nothing huge or anything. Just a little something I made to say thank you."

He opened the box carefully, and his eyes lit up when he saw what was inside. "Will you help me put them on?"

"Of course!"

They were similar to the gifts she had given Gary, but she had used some of the material from the peony dress to make these. The tie was a simple red tie, but the boutonniere was really astounding. She had made her father a peony boutonniere.

"It looks real! It isn't, is it?" her father asked.

"Oh no, it's silk. I made ones for Aretha, Gary, and Derrick too."
She looked around. She hadn't seen him since they had all arrived at the
huge tent where the show was being held.

"Speaking of Derrick, have you seen him? I meant to give him his
gift as well, but I haven't seen him since we arrived."

"I believe I saw him out front talking to all of the photographers."

"Ah, okay. There's no way I'm going out there now. People have
started arriving, and I don't want to have a full-blown panic attack."
She laughed nervously.

"I'll send him back when I see him, okay?"

"Okay, thank you, Dad. I've got to get back and make sure we are
all ready to go. The show is going to start soon."

"Will do. Have a great show. Break a leg—or whatever I'm supposed to say."

"Oh, definitely not that!" She laughed and hugged him again, careful
not to squish his peony.

Derrick found her a moment or two later. He had changed into his
suit and he looked absolutely amazing.

"Why, Derrick, my my, do you clean up nice!" she said as she
brushed off some imaginary lint from his shoulder. He was wearing a
black three-piece suit, similar to what Gary was wearing, but not a slim
fit cut. Derrick's was more of a traditional cut. "You look quite dashing.
But you are missing something! Wait here a second."

She ran over to where she had stowed the Berkin and grabbed
the last white box. She saw a flash of red and quickly covered it with the
cigarette case she used as a wallet and closed the purse. She even locked
it and tucked the key into her bra. She did not want anyone to see what
was in her bag.

She returned to Derrick and handed him the white box. "Here, I
made these for you."

"Thank you, Calli." He smiled and leaned over to kiss her cheek
before opening the box.

Inside were a second set of the peony boutonniere and tie. He looked
at Calli, excitement in his eyes. "When did you have time to make this?"

"Oh, a girl can't give away all her secrets you know." She smiled up at him, "Do you need help putting them on?"

"Yes, please. That would be great."

He quickly took off the plain black tie he had been wearing and put on the new silk one. She helped get it into the perfect position before attaching the boutonniere to his lapel.

"I think this is the best gift I've ever been given. Thank you, Calli." He hugged her tightly.

"I couldn't have done all this without your help. You've become more than just my dad's assistant, or friend. After the show is over maybe we can figure out what we want this to be?"

He was still holding her, her arms resting on his, his hands on her waist. Smiling, he leaned down to finally kiss her.

"Excuse me, but what do you think you are doing, young man? This woman is literally in the middle of her first ever fashion show. We do not have time for this right now." Aretha physically separated them and started shooing him away.

Laughing, Calli said, "Go on, the show is starting any minute now. You need to go find your seat."

"Okay, well that is to be continued later," he said, laughing over his shoulder as Aretha pushed him from backstage to the front.

Calli just shook her head as she grabbed a bottle of water and took a drink. She had been running around for the last few hours making sure all the models were dressed and ready to go. They all looked spectacular. The barely there makeup and natural ethereal style of hair matched the dresses perfectly.

Aretha walked up to her and, seeing the smile on her face, asked, "What?"

"Oh, nothing. I'm just taking a moment to enjoy this. Seeing everything come together like this. It's been an amazing gift, Aretha. I can't thank you and Gary enough. I think Mom would be very proud."

"I definitely agree! And let's take a moment to look at you! I'm so happy I had this dress cleaned. I had no idea you'd be wearing it today."

She was wearing the black Chanel dress they had picked out together and she had worn to that first disaster dinner with her father. "This dress is just classic, you know? I absolutely love it." She nudged Aretha lightly with her shoulder. "I did my hair and makeup all by myself. And Gary told me it looked perfect." She beamed brightly at

Aretha. The happiness she was feeling was apparent in her smile and the way her eyes sparkled.

"You look absolutely perfect. I wouldn't change a thing, except maybe putting one of the wonderful peonies in your hair." Aretha reached over and touched one of her curls. "Alright, you, let's get this show started! Finally! Twenty plus years in the making." Aretha laughed and pulled Calli to the entrance to the stage. "Are you ready?" she asked, quickly giving Calli one last hug.

"I think I am."

"Good luck, dear. I'll see you out there in a moment." She touched her cheek fondly before darting away to go to the front of the building.

The models had all lined up behind her and were ready to do their walk. They all mouthed words of encouragement to her.

Calli turned and took a giant breath before slowly letting it out. Then she pulled back the curtain and walked out onto the runway.

Chapter 26

The bright lights blinded her, but only for a moment before she was able to see all the people amassed. She took another deep breath, searching the crowd for her friends and family. Aretha and Aunt Maggie's outfits both made them stand out in the crowd. They were front row and center.

She waved when she saw them, then took yet another breath and raised the microphone up to her lips.

"Hello, everyone! I know none of you know me—I'm Calliope, or Calli, Morgan, Gabriella Morgan's daughter. I just want to thank you so much for coming to this little show for my mom. She was truly the most magnificent and wonderful mother a girl could ever wish for. I'm so proud to be showing you her work. Please have fun, as Mom would definitely want you to! This is for you, Mom."

She did a little bow before retreating backstage. Standing right by the entrance of the runway, she waited to hear what the response for the first dress would be. It was the sweet pea dress. She could hear the murmur of the crowd as the model walked down the runway.

She could not tell if it was happy murmurs, or unhappy ones, but she could not think of that now. The next dress was the fuchsia dress and, as the model walked down the runway, she could hear excited murmurs.

The next dress was the tulip dress, which was and one of Calli's favorites from the collection. She smiled at the model before turning to go find Lydia. They had about ten to fifteen minutes to get her ready.

Lydia, thankfully, was already wearing the red peony dress. "Oh my, Lydia, you are a goddess! Thank you so much for getting everything prepped."

"This dress is fire! Seriously. I cannot wait to hear the crowd's reaction. When did you have time to make this??"

Calli laughed. "I haven't slept much in the last few days, to be perfectly honest. But it looks great, right?"

"Oh! Absolutely!"

"Thank you, Lydia." She smiled and handed her the white box she had set on the stack of totes earlier. "Here. I made this for you."

Lydia took the box and opened it quickly. Inside was another one of the peony barrettes, this time in the same fabric as the red peony dress.

"Oh, it's absolutely gorgeous, Calli. Thank you! Will you help me put it in my hair?"

"Yes, but I need to go get changed so we have to hurry."

Lydia bent down so Calli could place the peony barrette in her hair. They had decided to have Lydia wear her shoulder-length hair in loose romantic curls. Pulling up the side for the peony sealed how perfect the overall look was.

"You look amazing. I'm so proud to have you wear this dress."

"Oh, thank you! This is seriously a dream come true for me. Now go get changed before the clock strikes twelve!" She giggled.

Calli went to change. Of course, she had been cool as a cucumber earlier, but now that she was about to wear the dress that she had made for herself, she was incredibly nervous.

Grabbing the garment bag, she gave the new dress a final look over before she darted into the changing room. She shimmied out of the Chanel dress and slipped the new dress on. She gave herself a quick look in the mirror, making sure everything was in its place before she stepped out.

She quickly grabbed the Birkin purse and brought it over to where the models were waiting to go out. The model in the white rose dress had just started her walk down the runway.

The last dress to go out before the peony dress was the rose dress. The model was absolutely beaming as she knew what was about to follow.

Lydia came to stand beside her, a calming force through all the frenzied activity. "Don't be nervous. If you are nervous, then I'll get nervous. And I can't be anxious or nervous when I'm walking in this beautiful dress. They will all love it!"

Lydia hugged her again, tight. "You really do give the best hugs," Calli said as she squeezed her back.

"Ditto." Lydia rested her head a moment on Calli's.

They both took a breath as the model wearing the red rose dress started the walk down the runway.

Calli laughed as they both pulled away. "Okay, your turn. Make one pass on the runway, and then I'll join you for a second pass, then we will all walk out again in a line."

She turned to all of the models grouped behind them. "Thank you so much for coming tonight. This means the world to me and to my mom. I know she's dancing up in heaven watching all of you walk the runway."

She shooed Lydia down the runway. She could not take the anticipation any longer and peaked her head out behind the curtain.

The looks of wonder and shock on all of the faces in the audience made the entire experience worth it for her. It looked like Aretha had almost fainted when she saw the red peony dress, she was fanning herself with a pink and leopard print fan. Gary, who was normally very stoic, actually looked incredibly excited, which made Calli ecstatic.

Aunt Maggie's jaw was wide open in shock. She had seen all of the looks as Calli was making them, but seeing them on the models in action was a completely different experience.

Her father and Derrick were talking furiously, their heads bent toward each other. Calli wondered what they were talking about, but as she saw Lydia reach the end of the runway and turn back, she knew she had about ten seconds.

She quickly grabbed her Birkin and pulled out The Shoes. She heard a few of the models around her gasp. They had seen the silver stars sparkle in the lights backstage as she put them on. Some of them knew exactly what they were. Their eyes went wide but they did not say anything to Calli. They trusted her.

Immediately, she felt the confidence she had been missing since she put on her dress come rushing back as she put one shoe on and then the other. Closing her eyes, she took just a second to revel in the feel of The Shoes on her feet. She could not explain it, but it truly felt like she was home. That this was what she was meant to be doing.

As Lydia reached the top of the runway again, she reached out her hand to Calli. "Come on, girl. Let's show them the real you, shall we?"

Calli nodded and stepped out into the bright lights of the runway.

This time, Calli did not stop as she came out on to the runway, as she was prepared for the bright lights this time. However, she was not expecting the roar of the crowd as they first realized she had changed her dress completely, but also that she was also wearing The Shoes.

Calli was wearing a shorter, more playful version of the red peony dress. It still had the same bustier top, but the full skirt hit just above the knees.

Lydia squeezed her hand as they continued walking hand in hand down the runway. She could feel the eyes of every single person in attendance on her. A million thoughts raced around her head. *Did I make a mistake? Should I have not worn The Shoes? OMG what if I fall? Do they hate all the dresses? Oh my gosh, what have I done?!*

But she felt steady and sure as she walked down the runway. Lydia was the steadying hand that she literally needed. As they reached the end of the runway, they both let go of each other's hands, and Calli let Lydia walk in front of her.

Lydia made a point to show off the pockets included in the dress as all the other models had done. She reached the end of the runway and did some fierce poses for the photographers while Calli stood demurely to the side. Lydia then motioned for Calli to join her.

She was not a model or a professional poser like Lydia, but she channeled her mother for a moment, giving a fierce look to the cameras. She was so proud of what she had accomplished and she couldn't care less about what everyone thought. She was doing this solely for her mom.

After a moment of hamming it up for the cameras, Lydia offered her hand again and they walked back to the top of the runway. About halfway up the runway Calli almost tripped, the audience gasping as they saw her slip. But they all started clapping enthusiastically as Lydia's steadying hand helped her not fall.

They finally made it safely backstage, but Calli realized they had to do one more walk with all the models. She took a deep steadying breath and said, "Okay, ladies, let's wrap this up, shall we?" They all huddled together for a massive group hug before lining up to go back out on the runway.

Calli took Lydia's hand and squeezed it. "Thank you."

"For what?" Lydia shot her a questioning gaze while they waited for their turn.

"For not letting me fall!" Calli laughed.

"It's no problem! I know you would never let me fallm, so I just did what was right."

"Well, I appreciate that."

"You're welcome. Now, let's go knock this show out of the park, so to speak."

"Yes, definitely."

They walked out hand in hand again, and the audience roared with approval. They were all standing and clapping enthusiastically. Calli thought if she smiled any more, her face would actually crack.

As they walked back to the top of the runway, Calli could hear someone shouting, "Speech, speech!" But she could not pinpoint where it was coming from. It sounded suspiciously like her father.

She held up her finger and mouthed, 'one second,' so she could grab the microphone. Struggling to turn it on because she was shaking so badly from joy, she ended up running to hand it to her dad. He quickly turned it on and handed it back to her.

"Thanks, Dad," she said and leaned over to give him a kiss on the cheek before running back on the runway.

"Hi, everyone! Hope you all like surprises!" She giggled, the happiness escaping from her throat.

"All of the gowns were all designed one hundred percent by my mother. Even the peony dress. I found her sketchbook one night after my father had dropped off her memory box of their time together." She realized she was telling the audience way too much and had to reel it in. "Anyway, I was inspired by her drawings and all the work she put into these dresses. So I decided to make the peony dress she had designed. I hope you all love them as much as I do."

The crowd erupted into applause, and Calli blushed happily.

"Thank you again for coming out to see my mother's designs. It means the world to me."

She bowed again and then stood there a moment, her hands holding the microphone in front of her, to take in all the applause and cheering.

This, right here, was the absolute highlight of her life. Nothing would ever beat this moment.

Epilogue

It was a few days after the fashion show, and Calli had rented out Lucca's for a little impromptu 'Thank you!' party. They invited all of the models, makeup artists, and dressers. She could not have done this without them, so she wanted to celebrate them.

She stood up at the head of the table and tapped her wine glass with her fork, trying to get everyone's attention as the servers brought out the food.

"Oksy, everyone! Guys!" She laughed waiting for them to quiet down.

"I know I can never say thank you enough for everything each and every single one of you has done for me and my mom. This has been a truly amazing experience. Please enjoy this amazing food and have fun tonight. If my mom stood for anything during her life, it was to always, always have fun."

Derrick got up from his seat to come stand next to her for the toast she was about to give. Resting his hand around her waist.

"I would also like to announce that I have decided to stay here in New York and continue designing. I have a bunch of ideas..." She grinned as she saw the response from everyone as they all stood up to cheer.

Derrick pulled her closer to him, and she wrapped her free arm around him, then she raised her glass.

"To Gabriella Morgan. May you enjoy your time among the stars. I miss you, Mom."

They all raised their glasses. "To Gabriella."

Acknowledgements

To my husband, thank you for putting up with all my shenanigans while I wrote this. I appreciate you providing the constant snack delivery and water refills. I love you more than I could ever express.

To my family, most importantly my mom. Thank you for always reading what I wrote and telling me how good it was! I could never have done this without you.

To Glady. Without you, *The Shoes* would not exist. I miss you and our errand adventures.

To Melissa, my first editor and the original beta reader. Thank you so much for everything you've done for me. Seriously.

To Noelle, my editor. Thank you for helping me figure this out! I could never have done this without our little chats. I appreciate you more than you know!

To Brooke, my publisher. Thank you for taking a chance on me. I know I can be too scatterbrained at times, but I'm working on dialing everything in. Here's to many more adventures!

To all my beta readers: Amber, Janette, Tye, Sheila, Maya, Kayla, Ethan, Elizabeth, Joni, Patti, Michelle, Laura A., Heather, Corrina, Tammi, Laura L, Bridget, Miranda, Leslie, Ann, Stephanie, Terri, Katie, Vanessa, Jasmine, Tiffany, and Nicole. Thank you! You guys rock my socks <3

About the Author

Lily Hall has been an avid reader and writer since she was young. She can pinpoint the exact moment she became a reader. Her dad had taken her and her brother to the local library and told them each to find a book that was at least an inch thick. He promised them both that if they finished the book they had chosen, he would give them one whole dollar. Thus started her love of books. She never did get that dollar from her dad, but it started her love of books and the written word.

In high school, Lily Hall was frequently in trouble with her parents for staying up too late reading or writing. She has hundreds of lovelorn poems and short stories that will happily never be seen by the general public. But she still uses the writing exercises she learned from her high school English teacher to this day.

Lily now spends her time writing whenever she has a free moment. She tries to manage her time working and writing but also spending time with her husband and family. It's a constant work in progress.

Her first book *The Shoes* is just the start of her collection of stories to tell as she has several others—over twenty—floating around in her head. Her next four books will be coming soon!